INGRID WIDIARTO

Uyghur Stories

Ingrid Widiarto

Uyghur Stories

REAL-LIFE SCENES FROM XINJIANG

VERLAG Akademie der Abenteuer

Translated by

Ann Dechesne-Huntley
Tim Dyas
Louisa Greve
R. Hale,
Ingrid Widiarto

Impressum

Verlag Akademie-der-Abenteuer

Boris Pfeiffer, Pfalzburger Straße 10, 10719 Berlin

E-Mail: info@verlag-akademie-der-abenteuer.de

1. Auflage

Umschlaggestaltung und Illustration: Kris Kersting

Satz: Kris Kersting

Herstellung: Verlag Akademie-der-Abenteuer

Druck und Bindung: BoD GmbH, Norderstedt

www.verlagakademie.de.de

ISBN (print): 978-3-98530-066-2

ISBN (ebook): 978-3-98530-067-9

Printed in Germany

Content

Preface

The Silk Road – almost everyone has heard about it, but many of us in western countries have no clear idea of the Uyghurs and a land called Xinjiang or East Turkestan. And yet this land is a strategic focal point in Asia that should not be overlooked.

The stories in this book lead the reader directly into the everyday life of the Uyghurs as it was a few years ago. In ancient times, camel caravans traveled through the deserts and oases of northwest China, bringing with them precious goods and knowledge. Today the Chinese Communist Party holds sway. The economy is booming, industrial facilities and drill rigs are springing up like mushrooms, railways and trucks are roaring over the "New Silk Road" to Europe and back, but for the Uyghurs whose home it has been for many centuries, life has not become easier. They have been left behind at the wayside and relegated to the fringes of society.

The term "Uyghur" means "united" and goes back to the time when a number of various Indo-European, Turkic, and Mongolian tribes living in Central Asian affiliated and founded in 744 AD their own empire: the Uyghur Khaganate. It extended far into present-day Mongolia, but later the Uyghurs were pushed back to the west and returned to their homeland, mainly into the Tarim Basin and Dzungaria. After a long and eventful history under various kingdoms and invasions from outside, the land was subdued in the middle of the 18th century by the Qing Dynasty and in 1877 incorporated definitively into the Chinese Empire. During the turbulent times after the fall of the Qing, the Uyghurs twice proclaimed an independent Republic of East Turkestan, but in 1949 the People's Liberation Army took over the land.

The population did not resist. They welcomed the Communists who promised to bring peace and justice after long years of instability and fear under the Kuomintang regime and a succession of contending warlords. In 1955, Xinjiang was awarded the status of an Autonomous Region, which means that the constitution guarantees the resident ethnic minorities some special rights and limited self-government.

Already in the 1950s, Han Chinese were settled from Eastern China to Xinjiang in order to secure and Sinicize this remote border region, to promote the economy and infrastructure, and to mine the rich mineral resources. Today, the Uyghurs are less than half the total population of Xinjiang, and they remain largely excluded from economic progress; the rights and freedoms stipulated in the Constitution and the laws concerning regional autonomy exist only on paper. The Han Chinese seize power and wealth; the Uyghurs are increasingly pushed to the margins of society and feel more and more restricted in their personal freedoms. Conflicts erupt repeatedly between the two ethnic groups, and always Uyghurs are blamed for unrest and violence. They are under general suspicion as potential terrorists. This prejudice is actively promoted by the government and media, further intensifying inter-ethnic hostility, and leading many Han Chinese to support harsh government repression targeting Uyghurs. Thus, ethnic tensions are pushed to a dangerous level. Hate and aggression are increasing on both sides and the strict approach of the Chinese policy is threatening to exacerbate the situation even more.

In the years after the stories in this book were written (prior to 2015), the situation in Xinjiang has deteriorated significantly. Ever since the publication of the „China Cables" at the end of 2019, international media have reported time and again about the so-called „re-education camps", the arrest of hundreds of thousands of Uyghurs and members of other Muslim minorities, about forced labor, forced abortions and the like. But very little is still known about the time before.

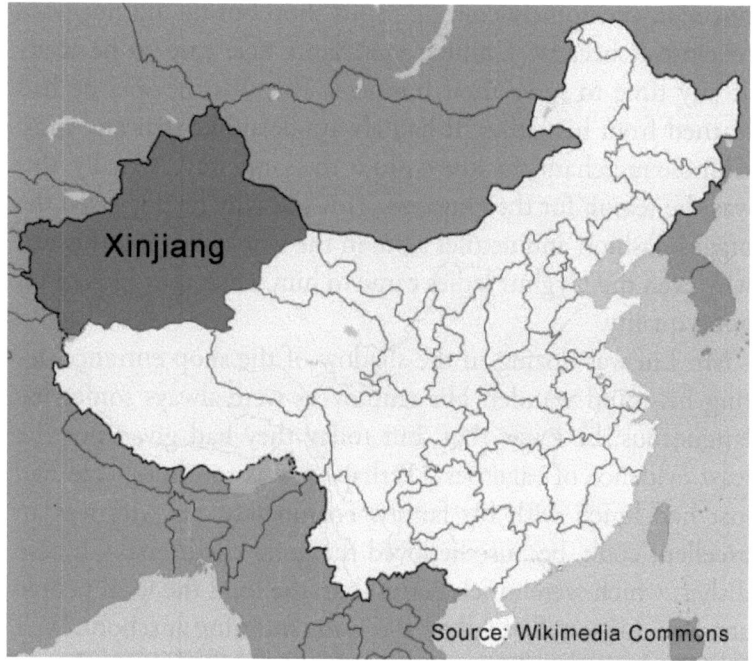

Source: Wikimedia Commons

Murat

It was in the early afternoon. Mr. Liu was sitting in front of his clothes store in the main street of a small town on the edge of the great desert. At this time of the day, there were not many customers coming to his shop but he did not want to close it because Chinese merchants take care to be ready at any time to serve their business. This was the way he had learned from his father. It had always been like that and most Chinese merchants he knew did it the same way. Actually, this was the reason for their success. This was why he possessed the biggest fashion and textiles store in the whole city and this was why even the Uyghur ladies came to him when they looked for good quality.

Mr. Liu was dozing in the shadow of the shop entrance, letting his mind wander. His employees were always somewhat languorous, he knew that, but today they had given not the least evidence of eagerness. Perhaps it was too hot.... He had just had lunch with his family. Fortunately, his wife was an excellent cook, because he loved the good traditional Chinese dishes, which were much better than the food the local people ate. Bao, his son, had talked about the morning at school. Well, actually he had to leave now for the afternoon lessons. It was high time. What was he doing? Lunch break must be over by now. Doesn't he watch the time? The boy is just lacking discipline! Mr. Liu got angry. Formerly we young people were different. We always knew what our duty was and did not linger about. Formerly... Yes, formerly in China...

Formerly in China... Mr. Liu quite often let his thoughts go back to the China of his ancestors, this big and mighty country far to the east, previously the Middle Kingdom and today the People's Republic of China, to *his* country, his *homeland*, this country which was governed so effectually that it would soon outstrip all other countries of the world. He himself had never been in this China. He knew it only from hearing the stories told by his parents. They had come to Xinjiang a long time ago, at the time when Mao had sent people from the East to these remote regions, because he wanted them to be populated by Han Chinese so that they could take part in the young country's progress. It had been Mao's well thought out plan not only to manage the economic development of even the most distant regions but also to Sinicize them from within. Thus, it would be easier to assimilate the native ethnic groups and to nip in the bud any recurrence of ethnic peoples' desire for independence. For this objective, many Chinese families had had to give up their homes. Mr. Liu's father had never entirely resigned to it. He had not liked this arid, desert-like country and had despised its inhabitants, who were so different from all those he knew. He had never stopped dreaming of the wonderful, fertile land in the East, of the sublime culture and the old stories. Up to the end of his life, he had hoped to spend his last days in the old homeland, but the government had denied it to him. He was buried now in barren, unloved ground, far from his ancestors' souls.

In the last few years, more and more Chinese people had come to this desolate country in the Northwest. They helped to push on progress and prosperity. There were lots of jobs. Everybody could earn good money and profit from diverse benefits and privileges. But the Uyghurs complain that they can't find a job, Mr. Liu muttered to himself. But why is that so? Why can't they find a job and get along decently, these permanently dissatisfied Uyghurs? Truth be told, the reason is that they do not know how to work hard, they are lazy and dumb. They might know how to take care of sheep and perform colorful dances, but getting the economy going and advancing industry, realizing progress, this they are incapable of. We Chinese we have to do it, and then they want to profit and never stop grousing. They grumble and complain because we are more effective than they are. Grumbling, this is all they can do, the Uyghurs. Yes indeed, nothing but grumbling, and at the end they blame us for making their life so hard! Isn't that the truth? – But what is the boy doing? He will be late for school after all! He is always making trouble! Oh, all this trouble everywhere!

Murat was fourteen and he was in a hurry to get to school. Lunch had taken longer than usual and now he had very little time left, if he wanted to reach the classroom in time. Wanted... of course he *wanted*, there was no question, actually he *had to*, because being late was unthinkable. He could not bear to be reprimanded. That was terrible, humiliating. Murat pedaled harder. Sure, sometimes a student arrived too late, but not he. Not Murat! He was always on time; he always did his homework, and always learned by heart whatever they had to learn by heart. Not because he liked it, but because he hated to be punished in front of his classmates. The least delinquency was penalized severely. After all, he did not dislike his teacher Abdureshid, who was a competent, upright man, but all teachers are bound to insist on strict discipline. No, he did not want to anger Mr. Abdureshid. And moreover – to be honest – it was great fun to bike like hell and find one's way throughout all the bicycles, mopeds, cars, carts and pedestrians.

Murat was indeed a skilled bicycle rider. He travelled between his parents' house and the school four times a day: early in the morning, before and after lunch time, and again in the afternoon when the lessons were over. His route led him through the middle of the town, first through narrow alleyways lined with clay houses and walls, then through larger, asphalted streets with bigger houses and high, shady poplar trees, and at last through the modern shopping street where there was considerable activity even at noontime. Only three or four minutes more, then he would have reached his destination. After that a few more meters and... Bang!

Murat got back on his feet with difficulty. His knee was scraped and his bike lay on the ground. Next to it, there was a second bike and a boy of nearly the same age, Chinese, who was trying to free himself from the tinny tangle at the wayside. What had happened? Had they crashed? A moment ago, his path had been completely free, Murat knew for sure. Maybe the other boy had come from the side, from a gateway or somewhere else where he had not seen him.

"What happened? Are you hurt?" he asked.

"No, it's okay," the boy answered while examining his leg from top to bottom. "Not so bad. And you?"

Murat set up his bicycle and noted with relief that nothing was broken. He felt a little dazed but he was about to hop on his bike at once so he would not waste more time. Bummer, maybe it was already too late!

"Sorry," he said, though he knew perfectly well that it had not been he who had caused the accident, but the boy looked so helpless and befuddled standing there by his toppled bicycle fingering his injured knee.

"Sorry," the Chinese boy also said. "It was too late when I saw you. I couldn't stop. I'm sorry."

Murat saw a man leaping out of the shop in front of which they had crashed. It was a well-known clothes store belonging to a Chinese businessman, he knew. Many people loved to go there. Even his mother sometimes stopped to look at the window display.

"I saw it, I saw everything," the man shouted flushed with anger. "Wait, you rascal! Wait! You won't get away with that so quickly!"

Foaming with rage and calling wild threats, the man came running to Murat.

"It was nothing, everything is okay," Murat tried to calm him.

He got a resounding slap.

"Please! Nobody is hurt..." Murat bent down to avoid the next blow but he had no chance. The infuriated Chinese man held him tight and hit him with all his strength. He hit him again and again until Murat lost his balance and fell down. The man grabbed his throat and knuckled it. He knuckled and pressed hard. His hands seemed cramped up around Murat's neck, and his face was distorted to a hideous grimace sparking with inscrutable hatred and implacable rage. Murat wriggled desperately. He could hardly breathe and thought he would choke to death. Then the man suddenly lifted his head and knocked it against the curbside. Again and again. Murat did not know how many times because he had lost consciousness.

He just regained consciousness when a foot kicked his head. A mean, hard kick against his head lying on the dusty pavement! One more kick, and another, without stopping. When Murat opened his eyes, he saw to his surprise that his tormentor was the Chinese boy who had some moments before been despondently examining his scratches. Now he stood next to the man who had choked him and you could see clearly that they were father and son, Mr. Liu and his son Bao. Confused, Murat noticed in a fleeting glance some other people standing nearby and watching. They were standing there in a row as if they were the audience at a theatre performance. Fast as lightning, he escaped the next kick. He protected his head with his hands. He rattled and coughed and tried to get up despite the pain.

At that moment, a new blow hit him on the head. Mr. Liu stood above him like a ferocious monster. An uncontrollable rage gleamed in his eyes. He seemed to be out of his senses with rage that contained so much more than anger with an adolescent who had crashed into his son's bicycle. It was rage against a whole people, against this barren land where he was forced to live, against a government that had sent his parents as well as many other Han Chinese here, under compulsion or with promises. It was a rage that had been built up by all the mistreatment and deception suffered over a whole lifetime. He was not aware of it, but he hated this Uyghur boy because he was in the right and his son at fault.

Indeed, how deeply a heart must be eroded by rage to erupt in such a blind fury, viciously beating up a defenseless boy. Murat was not strong enough to protect himself against the man. He blinked helplessly into the uncontrolled fury inundating him from glowing eyes. He gave in.

Just at this moment another student of Murat's school came across the street. His name was Turghun. He was some years older than Murat and known as a good soccer player, tall and in shape, admired by all boys of the Uyghur school. He immediately understood the situation and, without looking at the Chinese merchant and his son, came to Murat's aid.

"Are you okay?" he asked. "Can you get up?"

He reached out his hand and cast threatening glances at the assembled spectators.

Murat opened his eyes and tried to sit up. He was dizzy. Head, throat, chest, his whole body was burning like fire. He felt sick. He coughed and retched and gathered all his forces to buck up and not to collapse. With Turghun's help he got up, stretched out, smoothed his dirty shirt. To his astonishment he noticed that there was a policeman standing among the spectators. Had he been there all the time, watching? Why hadn't he interfered? How could he allow an adult to hit and kick a boy like him? He was just about to go towards the man and ask for his help, when the policeman turned around and went away. Totally taken aback, Murat watched him go.

"Come on, we will pay them back!" the soccer player prompted pugnaciously. "I'll take the old one and you the young one. Together we can do it."

15

Murat felt blood dropping from his right ear. When he touched it and saw his red smeared fingers, a panic-stricken fear took hold of him. Rage and despair suddenly overwhelmed him and in a blind fury he was about to pounce on the Chinese boy, who seemed to be again quite discouraged, hiding behind his father. But at this moment, one of the spectators tried to calm the situation.

"Stop! Wait a moment, boy," he shouted. "Let it be. It's not worth making yourself unhappy."

An old man, a Uyghur with a long gray beard and deep wrinkles in his face, who had seen the piteous spectacle, took Murat's arm and said in an appeasing tone,

"Let it be, boy. What happened happened. Let it be, and go to school now."

Murat wavered for a moment and looked at Turghun. He, too, had dropped his fists and listened to what the old man said, but a raging anger was still burning in his eyes. There was a profound bitterness, a fierce hatred crying out for retribution. Wrathfully he answered,

"Look at this weedy boy, Grandfather. And this one over there is an adult strong man."

"Please!"

"He hit him because he is a Uyghur!"

"Yes, I know, I know. But, please, let it be. Don't make a fuss of it. He is not injured severely." And to Murat he added in comforting words, "Your wounds will heal, my boy. Go to school now. Go and don't make things worse than they are."

Most of those who had watched the unequal fight were Chinese people, because the Uyghurs mostly lived on the outskirts of the town, in the small streets with clay houses and quiet creeks and trees. Now they turned away and left, because it was not a good thing to be mixed up in a dispute between Chinese and Uyghurs. They knew it too well. Nobody could predict what the consequences might be. Better to go and leave the

field to those who want it. Only Murat and the soccer player were still standing there looking at each other, not knowing
what to do. The store owner abruptly turned and disappeared
into his shop after he had given a good telling-off to his son.
Bao grumpily jumped on his bicycle and drove away. Probably he, too, had to go to school and would arrive late. Just like
Murat.

Teacher Abdureshid jumped up, startled, when Murat entered the classroom.

"What's the matter with you, Murat? What happened?" he asked, and all the students listened anxiously to what Murat reported. His face was swollen. He could hardly open his eyes.
His neck was covered with bloody scratches, his lips cracked
and sore. He tasted blood in his mouth and from his right ear
to his shoulder there was a thick, crusted trail of blood.

Lessons were forgotten, for such a hair-raising injustice concerned them all. They all were Uyghurs and they knew that the
Chinese thought themselves to be superior and regarded Uyghurs as second-class citizens, as an inferior people, backward,
uneducated, dirty. "Uyghurs have been kicked by a donkey"
was their saying. But how did they conceive this idea? Why
did they despise people they did not actually know? On the
other hand, the Uyghurs did not like the Chinese either, but,
of course they had a good reason for that. Because of things
like this incident with Murat. Because the Chinese were always judged to be right, even if that was not the case. Because
the government, the Party, the judges, all those who had a say,
were behind the Chinese and discriminated against the Uyghurs. Because, as their parents said, the Chinese had invaded
their land, exploiting it and forcing those who had lived here
for centuries to the margins of society.

"You should have clobbered him!" some students shouted.

"Silence, please!" Mr. Abdureshid urged. "Stop this stupid
know-it-all nonsense. Murat, go to the headmaster's office and

explain everything to him. And after that, go to the hospital and have your injuries checked!"

The headmaster wanted to handle the matter correctly. Someone would have to go to the store and let the owner explain himself, he said. The Chinese teacher should join Murat's father in order to avoid any language problems. When they arrived, the shop owner was very surprised to see them. He had no idea what they were talking about. Beaten? This boy? No, I have never seen him before. What happened to his face? It looks quite bad, poor young boy!

They were stunned, outraged. The man let all reproaches bounce off, as if nothing and nobody could affect him. As if he was immune to any accusation whatsoever.

"So we will call the police!"

"Okay, do that. Very good, I will be pleased to see the police and tell them what false accusations you are spreading against me."

At the police station, everybody was very friendly. Of course they would look into the matter. It was unacceptable that a simple bicycle accident should lead to such a brutal brawl. As a matter of fact, injuring an innocent boy must be prosecuted severely. Two policemen were sent out to arrest the accused.

"He wasn't there anymore," they reported when they came back an hour later. "We will go again tomorrow. Don't worry. We will take care of this matter. But... wouldn't it perhaps be better to forget it? It wasn't such a bad thing. Don't you think so? No?"

When, some days later, Murat passed the clothes store again and saw the owner standing in front of it, he felt his heartbeat stop, as if his heart would burst into a thousand pieces. For seeing this man and remembering his rage, feeling once again the pain he had suffered and remembering the wounds which still disfigured his face, made the blood freeze in his veins. He wondered, "What is he doing here? Why isn't he in prison?" And then he noticed the presumptuous glance! This self-assurance, this absolute certainty that nobody in the world could touch him, that power was on his side and that a Uyghur school boy should be very, very careful. All this was written in his face. Murat could read it like in an open book, though he had only seen it for a fraction of a second. But the sudden awareness of absolute powerlessness would haunt him forever and ever. His whole life.

Ghalip

What happened on July 5, 2009 in Urumchi?

Media around the world reported: "According to reports, 197 people were killed in violent clashes between Uyghurs and Han Chinese," using the figures provided by the Xinhua state news agency.

A vast majority of these victims were innocent Han Chinese, Xinhua said, but according to the World Uyghur Congress, many Uyghurs had previously been killed during the violent suppression of peaceful protests in various cities of Xinjiang. Demonstrators had protested against police inaction after the death of two Uyghur workers who were killed in riots in a toy factory in Shaoguan, Guangdong province. The protests in Urumchi had begun peacefully. People had gathered to demand an investigation of the incident in Shaoguan, but when the police began to attack the demonstrators brutally, violence erupted. The Uyghurs defended themselves in rage and despair, and finally not only demonstrators, but also many Chinese, died before peace could be restored. The anger was too great, the hatred on both sides immeasurable. Two days later, groups of Han Chinese joined together to take revenge on the streets. Bad things happened, very bad things that no one wants to remember.

Many young Uyghurs have since disappeared. Their families were given no information and were full of anxiety and sadness as they wondered, "Were they killed in the riots? Have they been arrested? Will we see them again?"

Like many other young men, Ghalip, a young journalist and blogger, has disappeared since those days. He had studied literature, published articles in various magazines, and worked in the office of a local newspaper. On a website of his own, he posted articles about history, culture and Uyghur society, and occasionally about political issues. Many readers throughout the country perused his posts with great interest.

It was hard for his parents to accept the idea that their son had been killed in the riots of Urumchi, but since he did not answer their calls and no message came saying he had been arrested or put on trial, they feared they had no choice but to say goodbye.

"He is dead," Mariamkhan said to her husband. He was paralyzed on one side from a stroke and had not been able to work for several years already. He had placed all his hope in the future of his only son.

"But he has not done anything wrong," he used to answer. "It cannot be that they kill innocent people. He has never done evil in his life."

Ghalip's parents lived in a small village near Bajingol. Other families, too, were missing someone they loved: a relative, a friend, a classmate. For some of them, death had been confirmed, others had been informed that the missing persons had been detained for terrorist activities. But Ghalip's family had never received any message. The only thing they heard after a few months was that he had been seen three weeks after the unrest in Urumchi.

"He was fine then," the friend assured them. "So he can't be dead." Mariamkhan burst into tears of relief and her husband's face was radiant with new hope. But what had happened? Where was he, and why was his phone disconnected? Why didn't he write on his blog?

Mariamkhan traveled to Urumchi. She went to police stations, government agencies, courts, the publisher. She asked everybody who might have once been in contact with Ghalip. But no one had seen him. No one had ever asked why he was not there, because so many people were no longer there. And no one had dared to inquire about him, because anyone who asked for a missing person would become a suspect themselves.

One year passed. Autumn came, winter came and then one day the secret police knocked at the door. They searched the whole house, asked who was going in and out of the house, whether someone had asked about Ghalip and what connections he had kept. They threatened to arrest the whole family if they did not report any person who visited them. They came only one time, but occasionally strangers were walking around, and who knew if they were tourists or spies?

And then a letter came, stating that Ghalip was in Shikho prison. He had been put on trial, sentenced to thirteen years' imprisonment, and transferred shortly afterwards to the north of Xinjiang. He was accused of posting fake news on his website and spreading separatist ideas. A call for separatism was a serious crime against the state. High treason.

Thirteen years were not a high penalty for a misdemeanor endangering state.

Thirteen years were a staggering high penalty for a young man who stood in the middle of life.

Thirteen years were thirteen years too much in a country whose Constitution expressly guarantees its citizens freedom of speech.

Mariamkhan was relieved and distressed at the same time. Her son lived, which was wonderful. But thirteen years in prison! It was hard to imagine such a long time, half a life. He was at an age to get married and start a family. He had a fiancée, wedding plans. Would the young woman wait for thirteen years? His life was still before him. He was a successful journalist and people wanted to read his articles. The Uyghur community needed men like him, men who looked behind the scenes and told the truth without agitating openly against the government.

She did all she could to see Ghalip at least one time and indeed she was lucky and got permission to visit him – for fifteen minutes. Mariamkhan, her husband, and daughter Adile were allowed to talk to him for fifteen minutes.

They drove to Shikho, more than a thousand miles away.

The weather was gray and nasty. Winter was approaching and here in northwest Xinjiang, the climate was much rougher than at home in Bajingol. They had not had much time to prepare a long trip, because the news had come so unexpectedly. Mariamkhan had just thrown some clothes into a small suitcase without caring for heat or cold. Then they had been on the bus for two days.

Now they were standing in front of the giant prison complex, far outside the city of Shikho, in the middle of the endless, desolate desert landscape. Bleak, threatening, forbidding. High gratings, thick walls, spotlights, sentinels. Hesitantly, they walked to the entrance and showed their papers. After they had been searched carefully, two guards led them briskly and with an emotionless, cool mien through long corridors. Doors were opened and locked again. The visitors followed as fast as they could. But as the two women had to help the old, disabled father, they fell back, so that the guards had to wait for them. Finally they stopped in front of a door, eyeing the visitors with a stern, ice-cold look and said,

"You have to follow the instructions: no touching, no unauthorized questions. Fifteen minutes."

Then the older man unlocked the door and let the family enter into a bare, windowless room lit brightly by two tubular lamps. The guards remained standing on both sides of the door while the visitors took their seats on three chairs in front of a grating.

After a while, a second door beyond the iron bars opened. A gaunt, bent figure in a much too big blue cotton suit, with a shaved head and lowered eyes, shuffled in, led by a guard. His arms hung limply from his body, his hands were tied.

"Ghalip," Mariamkhan wanted to call out, but her voice failed.

"Sit down!" one of the guards shouted from behind. Mariamkhan had been on the point of jumping up from her chair but was scared back to her place and slumped down like a scolded dog.

The guard on the other side of the grid led Ghalip to a chair and secured his hands with handcuffs at the back, and chained his feet to the front chair legs. Ghalip was still looking at the floor, as if his head was too heavy for the emaciated, meager body, or as if he was ashamed of himself and did not dare to look in his parents' eyes. Hadn't he brought disaster and disgrace upon them?

"You may speak now," bellowed one of the guards.

Mariamkhan straightened up, forcing her son by this movement to look up.

His deep-set eyes had lost any luster. His face was pale and blank. His whole body was emaciated, nothing but skin and bones, faded. He was nothing but a poor, helpless picture of misery.

"Ghalip," she whispered, shocked. And though it was a silly question and she hardly could control her voice, she asked, "How are you?"

He did not answer. For a brief moment he looked at his mother, then tears came into his eyes and ran down his hollow cheeks. He could not wipe them off, because his hands were tied, and before he had given his father and sister a glance, he bowed his head again.

What a lively person he had once been, full of vitality and enthusiasm, Mariamkhan thought. All this was gone, withered. He had lost his youth, his positive energy, his sense of justice. All that... where was it? Within a year Ghalip had become a completely different person, a person who was only a fragile, helpless wreck.

Mariamkhan was heartbroken when she saw him cry, chained to a chair.

Suddenly the father screamed and fainted. He slipped from his chair. The two women and one of the guards rushed to help, and laid him carefully on the floor.

"We'll take him to the infirmary. Come on, anyway, the time is almost over."

"Just a moment, please!" Adile begged. "Only one minute."

"Ghalip," she said to her brother softly. "Ghalip, hold on. We need you. We all need you. One day, Ghalip, someday you'll have to tell what happened. Do not give up!"

She had spoken Uyghur, and in case one of the Chinese guards understood this language, she added, whispering, "One day you must tell the world what they did to you, Ghalip."

"Speak loudly!" shouted one of the men immediately. "Whispering is forbidden."

Then they dragged the old man towards the hallway and closed the door behind the visitors.

Ghalip had not spoken a single word. What could he have said? If he had talked about the interrogations, all the terrible things he had seen, his fear, they would have immediately led him back to his cell, and he would have caused even more misery to his family. He already felt responsible for their misfortune. He had sacrificed them for a truth that should not be known as truth.

But it was the truth! He had not spread false news. He had written nothing untrue and he had not called for rebellion or separatism. This was the last thing he would have done, because everyone knew quite well what inevitably would be the result. He would never have risked that. But he did not want to accept the unnecessary brutal intervention of the police. The Chinese authorities were responsible for the bloodshed and to his mind, everybody should know it, because only then maybe someday something would change. If, however, all media in the world repeated the government's line that only Uyghur troublemakers had committed violence, attacking Han Chinese for no reason, and they alone were to blame, then *this* was a lie. Policemen had refused to protect defenseless Uyghurs. Hordes of Chinese thugs and paramilitary troops had bashed innocent bystanders and even hit them when they were already lying on the ground.

He had seen it.

He had seen it with his own eyes and he felt sick even now at the memory. He should have helped the boy, he accused himself for the millionth time. He wept, remembering the suffering in his mother's eyes, and he wept over himself, for he should have stopped those men with their clubs and helped the boy, but he had not done it. He had slipped away and typed a blog post on his computer.

This was also important, he had said to himself. With his bare hands he would not have achieved anything. He would have been beaten and arrested himself, and maybe he had done right to write the truth instead of impetuously giving help. But the scene of the boy lying on the pavement, in his blood, had followed him ever since with relentless persistence. At that time, he had made his decision. Nothing could be changed, and after all, the result was the same: imprisonment.

It had not been Ghalip's intention to provoke the government. He had only wanted to tell his readers what had really happened, and especially *why* it had happened. He had written that the Uyghurs in Xinjiang suffered from ethnic discrimination, religious restrictions, and economic disadvantages. They could not find jobs, their land was exploited, and all this because more and more Han Chinese were coming into their country and taking over everything. It was inevitable, he had declared, that under such circumstances grievances mounted and could burst out into the open at any moment. On both sides, so much hate and so many mutual accusations had been pent-up for years that it had now come to an uncontrollable explosion. The Uyghurs pushed the responsibility to the Chinese. The Chinese authorities blamed terrorist groups, incited by foreign separatists. This was the truth Ghalip had written. He and hoped to make both sides think about it, but it had brought him endless interrogations, anguish and thirteen years in prison. It had destroyed his life.

For Mariamkhan, life was not easier after the trip to Shikho. She knew now that her son was alive, but what life was it? He was reduced to a skeleton and his soul seemed to be broken forever. Nearly twelve long years were still ahead of him, twelve years of his life. She herself felt weak and sick. Her husband had not recovered from the shock in prison. He would soon die. She saw him languish without a will to live, without even making an attempt to get up from his bed. The sight of his broken son had broken him. The paralysis seemed to spread from day to day and a few months after his return he fell asleep and did not wake up again.

Mariamkhan did not mention his father's death in her letters to Ghalip. Anyway, probably he never received them, because she never received a reply. Therefore, no one would know what happened to him in the following years. Occasionally, some released prisoners reported the conditions in Chinese prisons and then Mariamkhan would imagine how her son's life might look like. Would he survive the thirteen years' imprisonment in his wretched health? In general, the prisoners had to do hard physical work. One heard terrible stories about it.

A man from a neighboring village had been convicted once for seven years in prison and in the end he received another five years of hard labor.

Probably Ghalip, too, had to toil in such a labor camp, up there in the north, where it was cold and harsh. Maybe on a field or in a quarry? Maybe he worked in the middle of winter in ice and snow knocking stones. She remembered the frail, weeping man who was tied by his hands and feet to a chair. He would not even be able to hold a hammer, he was so weak.

One day, a former prisoner reported that he had lived for years with eleven other prisoners in a cell with room for only six bunks, so they had to take turns. It is hard to believe, but it was possible to sleep standing up. Many people experienced terrible things during their detention, and it was impossible that they all invented tales just to make themselves important. A man from Hami had lived for forty-five days with twenty-four fellow prisoners in a cell that was just so big that they could all stand side by side. Only the corner with the toilet hole was left free for those who had to use it from time to time. Thus, they were standing all night in glaring light, monitored by a camera, sleeping or dozing, supporting and holding each other. Whenever one of them lost balance while sleeping, he got a thump from his neighbor, and fell asleep again. During the day, they had to work in a quarry, which was a hard, energy-sapping work. They were not strong, because in their daily soup usually swam only a few potatoes, but nevertheless they were happy every morning to go back to physical work, because they finally could stretch their limbs.

This man, who had gone through tough, painful interrogations and forty-five days under such incredible conditions, had worked as an engineer in a factory where one day a bomb had exploded. No one had assumed responsibility for the attack, but the police needed someone to blame and as there had been only two Uyghur employees, they arrested those two. After forty-five days their innocence had finally been proved.

Mariamkhan could hardly bear to hear such stories, and yet she wanted to know everything. Then she felt a little close to her son, hoping that he would survive. Every night when she was lying awake in her bed she wondered how his life might be, pent-up in a cell with many other men, each just a number, not a real person, sleeping, dreaming, hoping, weeping, eating, answering the call of nature, observed by a camera and under the constant threat of physical or mental cruelty.

One day he will be free, she consoled herself when she could not sleep. One day – perhaps she herself would not be alive any more – but one day he would be free.

Thirteen years of imprisonment for a blog.

Thirteen years for a truth that could not be exposed, because it would compromise the security of the People's Republic of China.

Is the truth really that dangerous? Or is it rather the lies and dissimulations that might one day have a subversive effect?

Hamut

It was July 7th, 2009, two days after the big demonstration. At the University of Urumchi the term was coming to an end. Only some exams and a practical course were pending, but since that terrible Sunday when the peaceful demonstrations in Urumchi and Kashgar had come to such a brutal end, everything was different, at the university as well as in the whole city. Nothing was the same. A paralyzing terror had settled like a dark cloud over the land, like a thundercloud which spread fear and fright with an invisible impending rumbling.

The students did not feel the usual happy anticipation about the upcoming summer vacation. They all waited anxiously for the latest news, desperately cherishing the absurd hope that this nightmare might not be true. That somehow everything would turn out to have a very simple explanation. They had been trapped on the campus for two days, protected by high walls and a horde of policemen. Of course, they knew that the rumors were true and that such riots could flare up at any time and everywhere in Xinjiang, because the Uyghurs had good reason to rebel against the injustice they were confronted with. Of course, they knew that there might be some violent Uyghurs who did things which one should not do, and they also knew that any resistance against the authorities, even an outspoken critical thought, was punished severely. So the students waited in a state of shock for what was to come. They hoped that the exams would soon go on and that they could complete their term without obstacles.

This morning, the president of the university announced that the government of Urumchi had come to the conclusion that order was restored and that it was no longer dangerous to leave the campus. Therefore, all students would be sent home for the vacation immediately. Everyone was to leave the city and return to their hometowns. Therefore one student in each class had to go to the train station and buy tickets for all his fellow students.

Hamut was selected for this task. At nine o'clock in the morning and with a lot of money in his pocket, he took the university bus to the main station. On his way, he noticed a strange atmosphere in the city. As the bus crossed the Uyghur district, Hamut saw unusual disorder, devastation, broken windows, dented cars, almost as if a wild tornado had swept through the streets. Anxiety, depressed faces, frightened children, Chinese soldiers wearing helmets and with machine guns slung over their shoulders. When he saw all these ominous signs, his own heart grew heavy.

"I entered the station with a sad face," he says to me in his somewhat clumsy German as we are slowly strolling through the quiet streets of an evening in Munich-Schwabing. It is easier to talk while walking, he had told me, and now I understand why he had said so. It is because of the tremendous tension caused by remembering something that he would rather forget. He looks at me with big eyes and I can still see a shadow of sadness in them. Maybe, five years ago, it had gripped his heart so deeply that it will never let in lighthearted gaiety again. We keep on walking for a while in silence, before he speaks again.

It was very busy in the main hall. Many young Uyghurs and even more Chinese people were waiting there. The line was so long that Hamut was prepared to wait for at least three or four hours. He would have to make the best of it and be patient. After all, he had to fulfil his duty, and if all students had to leave Urumchi, he said to himself, well, they all needed a train ticket.

Half an hour had passed when suddenly someone shouted near the entrance. A group of Chinese people rushed into the hall and others ran out. Hamut did not know what the reason was, nor could he understand what people were shouting about, but at least the queue had become much shorter. A moment later, twenty or thirty heavily armed policemen came in.

One of them knocked down an old Uyghur man, who stood in his way, and then ordered all those present to sit on the ground: head between the legs, hands on the neck!

"I could not do anything," Hamut says sadly, as if he had to apologize for not having defended a helpless old man against thirty armed policemen.

Then the police began to separate out all the Uyghurs. Hamut sidled toward a group of four foreigners sitting near him, perhaps Europeans or Americans, and asked them if they would allow him to sit between them, because he hoped that the policemen would not bother foreign tourists, but it did not help. The policemen fished him out and pulled him over to the other Uyghurs who were already lying on the floor, face down and hands clasped behind their heads. Then a policeman ordered the Chinese, who were still in the main hall, to remove all shoes from the Uyghurs.

"I turned my head to the side, because I wanted to see who was next to me," Hamut says, "and suddenly there was a dark shadow hovering over me, a thing so big..." He shows with his hands how big, and looks at me with almost disbelieving eyes. "A boot! It was a boot! And within seconds this boot kicked me in the neck and squeezed my neck mercilessly to the ground. I was so stunned that I began to laugh. I do not know what was going on inside me, but somehow I thought it was so stupid and ridiculous that someone kicks me, just because I had moved my head!"

"Did you really laugh? Or was it just a nervous laughing?"

"No, I was not nervous. I was not afraid. Not yet. And I did not feel any pain. I did not feel anything, because I was not in my right state of mind. For a brief moment I had seen something like a flash, as the boot came up, but actually I thought that everything was just stupid and I wanted to show this stupid guy who was so proud of his power how ridiculous he was."

But the result was not as he wished. On the contrary: the policeman kicked the man lying next to Hamut too, and even harder, much harder than him. He was bleeding from his nose and ears.

"Well, and if you don't stop laughing, my boy, I'll shoot you. Do you understand me?"

From that moment on, Hamut did not laugh any more. He would never laugh again. He felt miserable, because it had been his fault that another young man had been beaten cruelly. The muzzle of a gun barrel was pressed into his neck and he did not know what to think or feel. He had been terribly stupid and he would never be able to make up for it. He could do nothing but wait. Just wait.

Twenty-five Uyghurs, without shoes and with hands on their necks, were sprawled on the floor of the train station hall. Time passed. Maybe half an hour. Maybe less or more. Hamut had no sense of time and could not look at the clock, because he did not dare to move.

It was cold. Though it was summer and the sun was hot outside, a nasty cold came up from the floor and permeated his limbs.

Then finally someone commanded, "Get up! Line up in two rows!"

Hands still clasped on the neck.

A TV crew stormed into the main hall. A convoy of people ran excitedly back and forth, waving, calling orders to each other, cameras focused on the two rows of detained Uyghurs. A reporter said into his microphone,

"The police just succeeded in thwarting another attack. At the central station of Urumchi a group of young Uyghur terrorists was arrested..."

Hamut was in the first row and thought with horror, "My parents will see me. What are they going to think?"

"...a successful strike against the violence of Uyghur separatists and terrorists who were responsible for the death of countless innocent people during the past few days."

"Do they think I'm a terrorist?" Hamut marveled.

"The military and police are taking rigorous action against the insurgents who kill innocent Chinese at random. Hundreds of injuries are being treated in hospitals. But peace and order will soon be restored thanks to the courageous intervention of the security forces."

"Now we were brought out of the main hall, with hands on the neck," Hamut goes on telling his story. "Outside there were many Chinese who insulted us and spat. I felt wet spit on my face but dared not wipe it away, because I was afraid they might shoot if I moved my hand. It was disgusting. No one had a right to humiliate me. I had done no harm to anyone! I was just a student who wanted to buy train tickets for his fellow students.

"The police took us to another hall. It was very large. No one was there. It was completely empty. We had to stand in a line facing the wall, hands up. Would we be shot now? Yes, at that moment I was scared. No one would see it. No one would hear it. I really thought I was going to die."

For a while, Hamut walks silently at my side. I can hear him breathing, trying to calm himself. I feel sorry that he has to go through all this again because of me, but I am also very grateful to him, because how else could the world know what really happened in those days in Urumchi? The media report only the facts, not the feelings of those who are directly affected – and sometimes not even the truth. Unfortunately, I cannot give him any comfort. No one can. No one will be able to free him from the anguish that is still in his soul and maybe will be there forever.

The twenty-five Uyghurs were not shot. They were searched and interrogated. One by one they had to hand over their identity cards, all objects in their pockets. "Why do you need this, why that?" And so on. Hamut was the last one and it seemed that the interrogation would never end.

"Why did you come here? What are you doing here?" Over and over again the same questions. Hamut said everything he had to say: He had been sent by the dean of his faculty "Why? Why you? Tickets for whom? Where to? What name? All names please! Are they all students? Where did you get all that money from? Why were you chosen?" These questions went on and on for a long time until suddenly he seemed to have answered enough questions. He got back his money and his belongings and was sent away. Free!

Not dead, not arrested, but free!

The other twenty-four Uyghurs had to take off their clothes, were shoved into a police car and taken away. Hamut stood alone at the exit of the train station and looked after them.

"Oh dear!" he thought, horrified. "Better if they had arrested me too! It would be better to be in a police car or in prison than here alone in the street!" Everywhere there were Chinese people and they all looked angry. How could he get to the university? There were no cars, no taxis, nor the university bus. He wanted to phone, but his phone was not working. He would need to charge the battery, but at the place where he could have charged it, there were so many Chinese that he did not dare to go there.

Now Hamut was really afraid. He feared for his life. He was sure that against such a horde of enraged Chinese he had no chance of survival. But what could he do? He could not remain standing at the station gate. He had to return to the university, because only there was he safe. Maybe he could catch the bus in the Changjiang Road, then change bus somewhere...? A group of six Chinese men with clubs in hand came running up to him. He turned and ran. They followed him. He ran faster. They did also. He turned back to the station where he had seen some soldiers, because he thought, "better soldiers than furious, brutal Chinese." But the soldiers did not understand what he wanted and sent him away.

"I was very tired from running," Hamut says, now again out of breath. "But I had to try again."

On the way to the bus stop he heard somebody calling his name, "Hamut! Hamut! Wait!"

He recognized two girls from his university. How did they know his name? No matter. They were crying, they were desperate because they did not know how to get back to the university and asked for his help. Of course he had to help, there was no doubt about it, and together they tried to reach the bus stop. But when they came nearer, they did not dare to wait for the bus, because there were too many people watching them with threatening eyes, eyes full of hate.

"Let's go to the next stop. Maybe we can take the bus there," he suggested. But again they heard screams. A group of young men were calling, limping, bleeding, injured. One had a gash in his arm and was bleeding from his head. They were all smeared all over with blood. Helpless.

"They could not run with us," says Hamut apologetically. "We could not help them, because they were no longer able to flee. They were too badly wounded." And a little later he adds sadly, "I do not know what has become of them. I do not know if they are still alive."

At that moment they heard a loud roar coming closer. A whole group of yelling Chinese came rushing upon them with nail-studded sticks in their hands, agitated and threatening. Like Qin Shi Huangdi's armies, it seemed to Hamut, when they swept across the continent two thousand years ago with lances and halberds to subdue all rival empires. Hamut and the girls turned on their heels and ran back to the train station, where there were soldiers. In the vicinity of soldiers they might be safer, at least for a little while.

"Why were all these Chinese men acting so aggressively?" I ask Hamut. "I know that the media placed sole blame on the Uyghurs for the violence of the past days and that the Chinese were enraged about that, but the fact that so many of them went onto the streets to take revenge with their own hands, almost hunting Uyghurs, this surprises me."

"These people were not just ordinary citizens. I'm one hundred percent sure that they were not just normal people, but plainclothes police or militias who were given the order to take bloody revenge. That was intentional. That must have been planned."

"Hm."

"Do you know what nail sticks are?"

"No. A stick with nails, I suppose."

"It's like this, look." Hamut takes a small branch and draws lines in the sandy soil, because we are in a playground, where now in the evening there are no more children playing. "It's a stick like this, about four feet long, do you see? And at one end is a large nail projecting on both sides, so that you can inflict terrible wounds."

"Hm. Simple and effective."

Hamut takes a deep breath and then goes on talking.

"So we ran back toward the station. But it was pretty far away and the wild horde with their sticks and their archaic roar came closer and closer. 'Run!' I shouted to the girls, but they could not run faster. They were totally shattered. I knew that there was a police station in the area and if we could reach it, we would be safe there."

They reached it. The Chinese were no longer following them and Hamut banged on the door. Out of breath, trembling with fear, the fugitives waited a long time until someone finally opened.

"Go away!"

"Please, help us!"

"Go, get lost! We cannot help you."

Aghast, Hamut looked at the weeping girls.

"Didn't you hear me? Get lost, I said. Immediately."

The door was slammed with a loud bang.

On the way, Hamut had seen in front of a big business building in the Changjiang Road twenty or thirty policemen, and as the wild horde with nail sticks had withdrawn, he and the two girls ran as fast as they could in this direction.

"We were in a panic," Hamut says. "I did not think I would survive this day. We had already seen so much bloodshed. We were running like crazy, we had only our own safety in mind, but we had also seen what was happening around us. So much violence, so much suffering. An unimaginable sadness came over me when I thought that my parents and my brothers would have to live without me... But we kept running. We could already see the high building and the policemen in front of it. Without stopping we ran into the middle of them and out of sheer astonishment – or I do not know why – they all ran with us into the hall. Then we stood there exhausted, out of breath and confused. We were in a beautiful entrance hall. It was cool, spacious and splendidly decorated. We were safe! And so we stood there stunned for a few seconds and looked at each other."

"What's up? What are you doing here?"

"Please, let us stay here. Otherwise they will kill us."

"Who?"

"Those Chinese in the street."

"Why?"

"They are pursuing us. They are killing any Uyghur they see. We have seen so many dead and injured. It's terrible."

"What have you done?"

"Nothing. I had to buy tickets at the train station. The Dean sent me."

"You cannot stay here."

"Oh, please. Let's at least have a little rest."

"No, you cannot stay here. It is not allowed to just come and go here as you please. Leave the building at once, please."

We had almost reached the exit, when one of the policemen called us. He was a Uyghur. He had talked with his group leader and said to us,

"Okay, we cannot allow you to stay inside, this is forbidden, but you can stand outside next to the door. There you will also be safe. We'll keep an eye on you."

"I think this man saved our lives." Hamut breathes a sigh of relief." Let's have a break now, okay?"

Sure, my dear Hamut, we'll take a break now. He looks tired. Not just tired from walking and speaking German, but also tired from the memories of horror.

They stood outside the building for six hours.

Hamut does not tell me what happened during this time. It is more than he can bear. The sad look in his eyes tells me that I should not ask any more questions, that his willingness to talk about what he saw that July day five years ago is at its end. It hurts too much.

We go back to our friends, drink tea and talk about football, music and other things. Late in the evening when we are alone again, Hamut finishes his story.

"There was a small car at the roadside with shattered windows and a battered roof. The Uyghur policeman told us that a young couple with a baby had been in it. Some Chinese youngsters had stopped them and beaten them with sticks. They had screamed for help, the child had cried terribly, bled, but they could not intervene because he and his colleagues had to guard the building and were not allowed to leave. Maybe they were now on the way to hospital. But perhaps they were no longer alive."

Everywhere they saw Chinese men with clubs or nail sticks. Whenever a Uyghur showed up, they pounced on him like a pack of wild wolves. Once Hamut wanted to help a young man, who was being attacked by more than twenty Chinese, but the Uyghur policeman stopped him. "Stay here!" he said. "If you go, they will beat you too. Can't you see? They are beating everyone."

"My heart wept blood," Hamut says.

He and the two girls were safe, but they could not help seeing what was happening before their eyes. If he had been alone, Hamut would probably have let himself be beaten and killed rather than watching, but he had to protect his companions and bring them somehow back to the university campus. He stood there and was barely able to think clearly. There was no justice. No one could help.

At six o'clock, the police would stop work and go home. Then what?

What would they do then? In the streets it was too dangerous for Uyghurs, not only near the station and in Changjiang Road, but also in other parts of the city. All Urumchi seemed to be in a kind of homicidal rage, much worse than two days ago, said the Uyghur policeman. The Chinese were out of control. They wanted to see blood flow.

It was five thirty.

"We were terribly afraid," Hamut admits. But then, at ten minutes to six, a convoy of several black limousines arrived. Officials in dark suits got out and then a lady who seemed to be a very important person, maybe a minister. The police group leader came from his office and greeted the woman with great respect. Hamut summoned his courage. If they wanted to survive this day, he had to do something. Time was running out. They would never be able to reach the university alone on foot or by public bus. That was impossible. So he went to the lady, introduced himself and explained the situation. The Uyghur policeman confirmed what Hamut said. The others watched in silence.

"Please, help us!"

The woman had listened attentively, then she turned to the chief officer,

"Call the head office and order a car to take these three students to the university!"

A few minutes later the police car was there. Hamut said goodbye and thanked the woman and the Uyghur policeman who had both saved his life that day.

"We got into the car," Hamut tells me with relief in his voice. "We were not allowed to look outside. We had to put our heads between our legs and hands behind our heads, but nevertheless we saw what was going on in the streets. It was awful! Everywhere were Chinese rowdies. They all looked alike: all had the same haircut, the same nail sticks. The driver swore at us all the time. He was angry that he had to drive us, us Uyghurs. A Chinese man who had to serve Uyghurs! He would have kicked us out. Once, halfway, he stopped and told us to get out and walk the rest on foot, but we did not listen. We just stayed where we were."

After half an hour they reached the university.

"It was a miracle," Hamut concludes with a faint smile. "The two girls were crying like waterfalls and suddenly I felt terribly hungry. I had not eaten or drunk anything since breakfast. The whole day long I had not noticed it because I had forgotten everything but survival. I was sure I was going to die."

It was like a miracle, Hamut had said. But actually it was a nightmare and this nightmare is still deep inside him. The violence, the helplessness, the blood, he may never be able to forget. And why did it happen? Because some were Chinese and some were Uyghurs? Why was there so much hate? Even if, two days before, some innocent Chinese had been killed or injured, one could not punish all Uyghurs just because they belonged to the same ethnic group. Where did this boundless hatred come from? Was it because state television in Xinjiang had replayed scenes showing incidents where Uyghurs beat or killed

Chinese? Were mass media used to stoke racial hatred and thus justify the wanton killing of Uyghurs on the streets, whether by enraged Chinese mobs or plainclothes militia?

Ten days later the university sent eighteen buses to take all the students to Hotan.

"To Hotan?" I ask. "I thought you are from Ghulja."

"Yes, but we all had to go to Hotan, almost 1,500 kilometers to the south, through the entire Taklamakan Desert. All of us."

"Why?"

Hamut looks at me as if I were not quite right in the head, to ask such a question. Nobody asks questions, when something is decided from above. And who has to decide such things? Well, the party secretary. He can decide everything. He can even decide what the president of the university has to do, even though, ostensibly, he holds the highest position in the university. And if the party secretary decides that all students should go to Hotan, then all the students go south, even if they want to go north. It's that simple. Later, from Hotan, they can go wherever they want.

Hamut did not tell his parents what he had experienced. They wondered why he had become so quiet and pale, why he did not eat and left the room whenever someone turned on the TV news. But he said nothing. He had not been injured that terrible day, but his soul was deeply wounded. He could still see the blood on the street. So much blood. And his thoughts went back to all those who had been killed, wounded or arrested during those days in July 2009.

Five years had to pass before he was ready to talk about his experience.

Kurbanjan

When Kurbanjan turned on the television in the evening of October 12, 2009, he heard the following message: "The Municipal Court of Urumchi has pronounced judgment on a first group of Uyghur youths who were arrested during the bloody riots in July. Six were sentenced to death, one to life imprisonment." As the names were read, Kurbanjan stopped breathing. Thunderstruck, he stood in front of the screen. He knew one of these boys! He had been his pupil, a model student, friendly, attentive and diligent, appreciated by all teachers, and it seemed to be absolutely absurd to believe that this promising young man could be guilty of murder.

Niyaz Sultan was twenty-one years old. He had just finished his studies at the College of Education and was looking forward to working in a primary school in his hometown of Namelum. This had always been his dream. He wanted to work with children and to ensure that they grew up to become good, responsible people. He knew about the importance of the early years in a person's life. He knew that warmth and love, understanding and openness, are essential preconditions if you want to raise children to be upright people, and above all, he knew how important this was in modern society where everybody was pursuing his own wealth and power and where the coexistence of Uyghurs and Han Chinese was getting more and more problematic. Social justice, environmental protection, preservation of cultural values and traditions were pushed aside. Yes, Niyaz had big dreams. He wanted to help to improve the world, and to achieve this, his parents had given him the soul and his teachers the knowledge.

One day before the 5th of July, when Urumchi sank in dreadful tumult and aggression, Niyaz had said goodbye to his mentor Kurbanjan. He had already packed his belongings, because now he was no longer a student and could no longer live on the school campus. He had rented a small room in a guesthouse nearby, for he was not allowed to leave Urumchi until he had received his certificate and leaving papers, but they were not yet ready. If the school administration had had them done on time, Niyaz would probably be today a happy young man who guided many happy children on their path through life.

But that's not what happened.

On Sunday morning Niyaz was sitting with some friends in the courtyard of the guest house. They all knew about the demonstration, which had been announced by various internet platforms and blogs. After all, people had to protest publicly against the repressive and autocratic actions of the security forces, against the constant show of force by the Chinese government, and against the unfair treatment of members of the Uyghur ethnic group. Recently two Uyghurs had been killed without intervention of the police. The police intervened only when Han Chinese were threatened, because it always seemed to be a foregone conclusion that the Uyghurs were the culprits and never the Han Chinese. All those who were sitting in the little courtyard knew it and all of them had experienced such a situation or knew someone who had experienced it.

They thought it was correct that at last something was being done. We cannot just resign ourselves to everything, they said. We should not put up with all this injustice without resistance, because we have a right to equal treatment. All ethnic groups in the country have the same rights and even though our land belongs to China, it is still the home of the Uyghur people. It is right to stand up for this in public. However, as for taking part in the demonstration, that was a different matter. They discussed it for hours and could not come to an agreement. Some of them finally decided to go.

"It is our right and our duty to stand up for justice," they said. "There is no other way for us but a big demonstration with as many people as possible."

Others hesitated. Occasionally one heard that even in central China, protests were crushed by brute force. The official media did not report such incidents, but there was the internet and the young people knew much more than they were supposed to know. They were quite aware that it was risky to join this great demonstration and therefore they had to think it over carefully.

And others, including Niyaz, did not want to have anything to do with it.

"Of course, it's true," he admitted, "that we Uyghurs have a right to defend ourselves against discrimination, but I will do it in a different way. I will not fight and demonstrate. I want people to develop a sense of justice in their heart. I want children to learn from an early age how to live together in friendliness and peace. That's why I became a teacher. I know I can achieve a great deal in this way, and I will not take the risk of getting arrested for showing my opinion openly in the street. Then I could not do what I think is really important."

This was what Niyaz said, and he was sure that he had made the right decision. With a few friends he remained in the guesthouse until evening. Then suddenly they heard a terrified cry, then shouting, crashing sounds, cries for help, lots of people running in the street. The boys jumped up and ran out of the courtyard. Fire! On the other side of the street a house was burning. On the ground floor was a shop. Flames licked from its windows. The door was open and they could see the fire flaring up inside. Acrid smoke wafted toward them. People stood and watched the scene in horror.

"We must help," Niyaz called to his comrades. "Maybe there is still someone in the house."

He ran straight to the burning shop. Out of the door came a high flame. No, it was too late! If anyone was still on the upper floor, nobody could save him. It was impossible to get into the house. Everything was on fire. Niyaz held a handkerchief to his face and drew back a few steps.

A police officer grabbed him from behind on the arms. Handcuffs clicked and Niyaz was dragged away and thrown into a car. He did not know what had happened to him. He was stunned, his eyes were burning, smoke and heat everywhere, screaming, crying. He coughed. Wooden bars broke down, sparks everywhere, shouting...

"Niyaz?" He heard somebody saying his name. It was one of the boys who lived in the same guesthouse as he. A few minutes ago they had philosophized how to make a better world and now they were caught in a police car.

"Why are we here? Why have they arrested us?"

"Because we are Uyghurs."

"We have done nothing wrong."

Another voice came out of the darkness of the car.

"We are always blamed when something happens. No matter what."

"Nonsense, they will have to admit that we are innocent," Niyaz replied confidently.

A girl was weeping.

"They arrested everyone who looked like Uyghurs. Just like that, all Uyghurs who were in the vicinity. I just wanted to get home. My parents are waiting."

Someone tried to calm her, but she could not stop crying.

The doors were slammed, the engine started, the young men and women were driven off to hell.

Nobody missed Niyaz in the following days. His friends did not miss him, because they believed that he had gone home. At school nobody missed him, because he had said good bye to his teachers. And at the office nobody paid attention to the fact that he did not come and get his papers.

Kurbanjan stood in front of his television, turned to stone, and still could not believe what he had just heard. Niyaz Sultan

46

had started a fire in the shop of a Chinese man and killed innocent people. Niyaz? No way could this be true! Niyaz would never do anyone any harm. Never! As he stood there, trying to bring some order to his thoughts, he remembered that a few weeks after the big demonstration in July, the police had once called and asked him if he knew a certain Niyaz Sultan and what he could tell about him. At that time he had been astonished, for he could not imagine what this young man could have to do with the police. And later, he forgot about it. He had assumed that Niyaz was already living with his family and had started working as a teacher, as he had so long wished.

Kurbanjan could do nothing.

"We have to get out of this country!" his wife said. "How can we let our children grow up here where they can be sentenced at any time simply because they are Uyghur?"

Her husband looked at her uncertainly. Rena was always so quick! So radical. Of course, she was right that repression was increasing and Uyghurs were often treated unjustly. Everywhere Han Chinese were favored. At work, even in finding employment, Uyghurs rarely got a job in the big state-owned enterprises. And where you could make big money, in the desert oil fields, for example, or in the mining of rare minerals, not a single Uyghur was accepted. There were only jobs for Chinese people. And as far as the *Bingtuan* was concerned, these insulated "little Chinas" within Xinjiang, which took away the best land and drained the precious water from Uyghur land, local people were hardly ever allowed to enter. In public services, which according to the Constitution should be headed by members of the ethnic minority of the respective Autonomous Region, Uyghurs mostly held only minor positions or were subordinate to Chinese functionaries. He knew a well-trained Uyghur engineer who worked on the assembly line, while his Chinese superiors could barely distinguish a screw from a nut. Now it even seemed to be difficult to find a job in a kindergarten or primary school. Many of his graduates had come to him with tears in the eyes, because all their applications had been rejected. Even though their diplomas were excellent, they were told again and again: "Your Chinese is not good enough."

He himself, Kurbanjan, had also been victim of the constant discrimination; he was a lecturer in Uyghur literature, but since the Uyghur language was gradually disappearing from school education and students had to speak Chinese, he was not needed anymore. In the coming school year he would just have to sort books and dust the shelves of the library. His knowledge was no longer of interest.

But leave home because of that? Start a new life?

Kurbanjan avoided his wife's gaze. He did not want to talk about it now. He was completely taken aback by the news and he really did not want any more problems at the moment. Why did Rena always come back to this issue? She always wanted to settle everything immediately. She hated compromise. He did not. He thought that compromises were far less strenuous than decisions. And how did she plan to put all this into practice? That was not an easy thing. Sure, once he had learned some German, but what would he do in Germany and how could he get a visa for himself and his family? And an exit permit? These were questions that gave him a headache, even before he asked them.

"The poor boy," he said casually in order to divert her attention from the annoying subject.

"Scandalous injustice!" His wife fulminated. "Did he have a lawyer?"

"How can I know?"

"I guess no. A man condemned to death without a lawyer, without witnesses, without evidence... A thing like this can happen nowhere but here!"

"Rena, please."

"No way, 'Rena, please....' Our life cannot go on like this, Kurbanjan! Try to get a visa for Germany. Please, at least, have a try!

Do something! Then we will come to visit you in the summer holidays and stay there. Or in another country, in Sweden, for example, or in Norway. Many Uyghurs have been granted asylum there. Think about the future of your children."

Again Kurbanjan's thoughts went back to Niyaz Sultan.

"Poor boy."

"The poor boy could be your son!"

At this moment a blow hit him like a flash of lightning from the blue sky and made his whole little world crumble into a hopeless nothing. He sat down on a chair and said nothing. This was not unusual, because he always sat down on a chair and said nothing when he tried to avoid further discussion. He could sit for hours like this. He never spoke much. Everyone knew him as a quiet, reserved man who preferred to let others talk. He listened patiently when his wife spoke, but he preferred to keep silent. Now, however, his silence had a very specific reason; he needed to think. For a brief moment he had seen his fourteen-year-old son Yasim with bound hands, a black cloth over his eyes, machine guns aimed at his chest; he had heard a fusillade and then nothing. Nothing. Only a senseless, futile emptiness. At that moment he had sank onto his chair and begun to search in almost panicked helplessness for a way out. His wife had long shown him the way, but now he needed a concrete solution, a path that led him out of all this madness of prejudice and injustice. And he had to find it now. Right away!

"Do it for your children!"

Kurbanjan did not answer. He left the room without a word and sat down at the computer. Tonight it was too late to submit an application, but he could start to formulate a letter, to think about possible justifications for leaving and to develop a strategy. There would be much to do. Tomorrow morning he would speak with the headmaster, who would be quite happy get rid of him. After all, he did not need him as a literature teacher any more.

The next morning Kurbanjan continued to work on his application. It would not be a problem to get a release from work for a one-year stay abroad. He just had to look for a university in Germany that would offer him the opportunity to study German children's literature. For what purpose, that did not matter, that was completely unimportant. The important thing was to get a passport and a visa for Germany.

Later in the morning he tried to call Niyaz's father in order to express his compassion. The boy had often mentioned his father because he wanted to be like him. His parents had always been an example for him. He had learned from them what was important in life: kindness and openness. If all children had parents like them, the world would be far more peaceful, he used to say. But as this was not the case and as he knew the educational methods in Chinese schools and kindergartens – discipline and more discipline, sitting still and obedience, obedience and sitting still – he did not want to become an engineer or scientist, but wanted to work as a teacher in a primary school and teach little children to treat each other with love and respect. Then, finally, these insane tensions between Chinese and Uyghurs would stop one day and all people could be friends.

Mr. Sultan did not want to talk to Kurbanjan.

"It's over," he said. "We have been waiting in vain all that time for his return. No one had told us where he was. We had no information – until the day of the trial."

Kurbanjan tried to say something comforting, but the other man did not want to hear it.

"And now he is dead," he ended the conversation.

The execution was carried out shortly after sentencing. Six young people had lost their lives, simply because they had been in the wrong place at the wrong time. And because they were Uyghurs. Some people living at the guesthouse, when they heard about the terrible judgment, later reported that Niyaz and his comrades had still been in the yard when the fire broke out, and that they had run into the street only when the noise had made them curious. But it was too late. They had not known that their testimony might have saved six lives. No one had ever known that the boys were in prison, and no one had ever asked for the truth.

For two more years, Kurbanjan tidied up the school library. He wrote letters and petitions, sought to establish influential relations and bribe the right people. He shaved his beard because some officials considered beards as a sign of rebellion and religious extremism. He never missed even one of the many required political training sessions. Finally, he received a visa for a one-year stay at a German university as an exchange scientist. When the summer holidays came, Rena and the two children visited him. They traveled to Scandinavia and did not return. Since then, the family has lived in a country where they feel free, where the children are supported by the government instead of being repressed, where Rena can openly say whatever she thinks and Kurbanjan can remain silent whenever he wants to – though he has already mastered the new language perfectly.

Nurgul

t was near Kucha in a quiet suburb, where everybody did their work every day as they had always done: the artisans in their small workshops, the merchants in their shops, the farmers in the fields or herding their sheep. And the police at the police station opposite to Nurgul's house.

Here in the village, the old traditions were still alive and nobody paid much attention to big politics in the capital Urumchi or in far-away China. People were quite content not to be bothered with these things, for they usually meant no good. Occasionally news came. The children or neighbors talked about disturbing events which Nurgul did not like to hear. The news, however, which was broadcast on television, was always good news and if it was true, there was no need to worry about the future. Nurgul and her husband Barat did not have a computer and did not know much about the internet and all this modern technical stuff. Their children of course did, but they lived in the big city and led their own lives. She and her husband, however, loved the quiet, peaceful life in the village which protected them from the unpredictable storms of the world.

Early in the morning when Nurgul was preparing tea in the kitchen, she heard a sudden noise in the road. Shouts, screams, roars. Suddenly a bang. Another one. Then there was silence again. It had almost sounded like shots, as one occasionally heard in television films. Nurgul ran to the window, but there was nothing to see. It must have come from the other side, maybe from the police station. She ran to the front door and was about to open it, when there was again a wild noise. Cars screeched, men's voices shouting, screaming, howling. An unimaginable roar, a hellish noise came from the sky. Perhaps a helicopter, she thought. It came nearer and nearer, an incredible roar getting louder and louder. Nurgul stood petrified behind the door when Barat came to her, still half asleep.

"What's up? What happened?" he asked.

"I don't know. I just wanted to go out and see."

She reached for the doorknob.

"Wait!" Barat stopped her. "Let us stay in the house. It might be dangerous."

The helicopter seemed to have landed. The roar sounded different now. Another car squealed and men were shouting something. Then again shots, loud and very fast one after the other.

"Machine guns," Barat whispered, gripped by excitement and fear.

"I need to see what's going on, Barat. I must tell our boy. He has just recently talked about such an incident, do you remember? He will be interested to know that such a thing happened at our house. I must call him."

"Stay in the house, Nurgul! Please, do not go out!"

It was quiet now. The helicopter had turned off its rotor, there were no more shots and the men had ceased to scream.

"I'm going now," Nurgul decided. "I'll just say that I have to buy bread when someone asks what I am doing in the street."

"Better stay here, Nurgul. Later someone will tell us what happened."

No! Nurgul wanted to see with her own eyes what had happened in front of her house, because she had to tell it to her son. He had to know these things. He always knew everything.

She had the phone in her hand, when she opened the door and stepped out. She looked around and stopped dead on the threshold, scared and confused, because never in her life had she seen so many police and military vehicles. A dark gray helicopter stood in front of the police building. Men in uniforms were talking, gesticulating wildly with each other, ran back and forth, had rifles slung over their shoulders and were wearing helmets. And on the ground... there were people lying on the dusty ground. Blood. There was blood everywhere. Some of the people on the ground lay in pools of blood, they were dead, others seemed to move. Nurgul, who was still holding her phone in her hand, lifted it automatically to her ear, but she was unable to press the button, let alone say a word. Stunned, she stopped in front of the house and stared at this almost surreal scene. She had thought that these things could happen only in films, not in reality and not in her own small village.

A black cloth blocked her view.

Two men seized her arms and led her away. She did not resist, because she still was not totally herself. The sight of so many dead bodies had disturbed her profoundly. There had been at least ten, maybe even more.

With the black cloth over her head, Nurgul was led to a police car and taken away. No one said a word, no one gave an explanation.

"I need to talk to my husband," she hissed under her cloth. "He will be worried if I do not come home."

There was no reply.

"What have I done that you kidnap me?"

"Shut up. Later you will have enough opportunity to talk."

Nurgul did not want to make her situation worse than it already was and remained silent.

A little later she was sitting in an interrogation room. The black cloth had been taken from her, so that she could look around at her leisure. In the room was a table and two chairs, and from the ceiling hung a lamp that spread a harsh, cold light. Above the door a camera was mounted which probably recorded everything that happened here. But at the moment nothing was happening. She was alone. She sat all alone in this horrible bare room on a wooden stool. One of its legs was a bit too short, so that it shook at the slightest movement and made a small noise each time.

Nurgul sat alone on her stool and thought about what she had done. What had she done? She had heard shooting, fear, anger, cars and a helicopter and she had become curious. Was it a crime to be curious when a helicopter lands on your doorstep? Who in the world would not be curious? Can anyone tell me this, wondered the woman who loved nothing more than her quiet village life and her children. She had felt that something terrible had happened, violence and bloodshed, and she had wanted to report it to her son, because he had always said that such things should not happen. So she had to tell him about it. In the end, she had not called him because somebody had ripped the phone out of her hand and had thrown a black cloth over her head. So what did she do wrong, why did they put her here, making her sit in this hideous room?

She felt angry about so much insolence, but then the fear was even greater than her anger. Nonsense, she tried to calm herself, I need not be afraid, because nobody can blame me. I will say that I wanted to buy bread and nothing else. Everyone has to buy some bread in the morning, right? It was not my fault that there was a helicopter landing and dead people lying on the ground.

Nurgul sat and waited.

Then the door opened and three men entered. Two of them sat down on the chairs at the table. The third one remained standing beside the door. They all looked at Nurgul. No one spoke. Nurgul looked at the men and asked herself, "What now?" But she did not say it, she just waited in silence.

"Whom did you call?"

Nurgul winced. In what an insolent tone is this man speaking to me? Can't he be more polite? No one has ever talked to me in such a sharp tone and behaved so impudently. For a moment, she could only stare at the man in astonishment. Then she replied defiantly,

"I did not call anyone."

"That's a lie."

"No."

"You called someone. We have seen it."

"No, I did not."

Nurgul's mind began to work: If the men were so anxious to know whom she had tried to call, the things she had seen must have been something that no one should know, something secret. And if anything should remain secret, then it must be of the highest importance. And if something is of the highest importance for the police or the intelligence, it must be dangerous. And if it is dangerous, then I should not involve my son in it. Therefore, on no account, I can say that I wanted to call my son. And if they do not stop asking, I have to tell them something else. Of course, they will not stop asking. Just look at them, Nurgul, look at these men! Just see how powerful they feel.

"So, whom did you call?"

"I did not call anyone, because someone took my phone."

"And whom did you intend to call?"

"My sister."

"Why did you want to call your sister?"

"I was afraid. When I heard the noise in the street and the shots..."

"You heard shots?"

Should she not have heard shots?

"Well, the helicopter and so many cars... I was suddenly afraid that the Third World War had broken out."

The two men looked at her in surprise.

"And what does your sister have to do with the Third World War?"

"My sister lives in Sweden and she always knows what is going on in the world. So I wanted to ask her."

The two men at the table looked at each other. Nurgul was not sure whether they believed her. Was there amusement in their eyes, or was it rather pity for such a feminine simple-mindedness? Or was it anger at her bold lie? Perhaps she had invented a silly excuse. But, alas, it was really difficult to behave properly in such a delicate situation! How could she know what was best? In any case she seemed to have confused the men for a moment.

"What's your sister's name?"

"She has the same last name as me, Mammat."

"And her first name?"

"Maryangul Mammat."

"Where does she live?"

"In Sweden."

"Why is she in Sweden?"

"Because she moved there with her family."

"What is she doing there?"

"Well, what you usually do, as a woman, as a mother..."

"Is she politically active?"

"I beg your pardon?"

"Is she politically active? What exactly does she do? Does she work for a Uyghur organization?"

"I don't know."

"Why did you want to call her then?"

"I didn't."

"But you wanted to do it. So why?"

They asked and asked and did not stop. For hours and hours the men asked their questions and Nurgul gave answers that did not satisfy them. Again and again the same questions. It was cold. Her back hurt because the wobbly stool had no back against which she could lean. She got thirsty and hungry. She was tired.

"Why did you want to call your sister?"

"I didn't call her."

"What were you going to tell her?"

"I wanted to ask her if she knew something about a new war."

"Why did you think of war?"

Could she answer because she had seen the dead bodies? People shot dead?

Something inside her warned her against it, because she probably should not have seen them. Why else would they have thrown a black cloth over her head so hastily? So she should actually know nothing of the shooting. But she had to give an answer if the questioning was ever come to an end. Therefore she admitted,

"It was as if I had heard shots."

"Shots?"

"Yes, like sometimes in TV films."

"Ah," said one of the men.

"On TV," said the other. Nurgul said nothing more.

"Was your TV running?"

"May I go to the restroom?"

"No."

"Can I have a drink?"

"No."

"Did you have the TV on?"

"No."

"Where did the shots come from?"

"I don't know."

"Are you sure you heard shots?"

"I'm not sure of anything I heard or what I saw or did. I'm tired."

A wink to the guard at the door, a bucket of water swung at her and an icy flood of water spilled over Nurgul's head. Everything was wet, her face, clothes and feet, all wet and cold.

"Better now?"

Stunned, Nurgul glared at the men. Everything was dripping. She did not know whether to be shocked or frightened. She did not remember how it happened. Somehow the world seemed to be falling apart. All this could not be true. She had wanted to make tea for Barat and have breakfast with him. That was all she had wanted, nothing else... and now she sat here all day long and was doused with cold water!

The two men rose from their chairs and left the room. The guard at the door was again standing stiff and blankly staring in front of him. Nurgul closed her eyes. She almost lost her balance. At any moment she might fall off the stool, she thought, when suddenly two other men appeared. And it all started again. Again the same questions, again the same unsatisfying answers. Again a bucket of water.

From time to time she was allowed to drink a little water, and once she was led by two women to the toilet, but she was not allowed to sleep. She was sitting as upright as she could on the small, rickety wooden stool and tried to withstand the endless questions. When she was about to fall, the next flood of water sluiced over her and at the end she admitted that she had heard shots and confessed that she had seen corpses. Anyway, they knew everything. Why did they ask again and again? They must be pretty stupid, these men, she thought. Men who feel powerful, but slow on the uptake... But after all, it was not important any more. Nothing mattered. Let them do whatever they want. What's the problem? At least she had not involved her son in this matter and her sister in Sweden was safe, because she was no longer a Chinese citizen. Barat hopefully was all right at home. Oh, better if she had listened to him and had remained in the house! Again she could not keep her eyes open and again a bucket of water was poured over her. Wet is wet, she thought, what the heck? But what a senseless waste of water!

She did not know it, but she had sat nearly seventy-two hours on a stool answering questions. Or not answering, because she did not understand them. Now she found herself on an uncomfortable wooden bench in a jail cell and rubbed her burning eyes. She had slept. She did not know how long she had slept, but she felt hunger and a terrible thirst.

"Is there anyone there?"

When there was no answer, Nurgul dozed off again and fell into a deep, disturbed sleep. Confused, nightmarish dreams tormented her. She dreamed of war and floods of water, she heard gunfire, death wails and senseless questions. From time to time she woke up and looked around, confused. Was this a prison? Had they put her into a prison cell? Nothing was to be heard.

"Is anyone there?"

Nothing.

Suddenly she discovered a faucet coming out of the wall in the corner next to the toilet hole. With difficulty she got up from her bed. All bones ached, her legs were stiff, her back seemed to have grown crooked, her head roared as loud as a helicopter falling from the sky. "No!" she screamed. "No, not again! Please..."

She slowly felt her way along the wall toward the faucet, when suddenly the door lock began to creak and the cell door opened with a crack. A woman peeped in and asked, "Is everything all right, number 88?"

Nurgul looked at the door, surprised. A woman! A number 88! A woman asked whether number 88 was fine... She looked around, but since nobody else was in the room, she said,

"I'm going to the tap, I'm thirsty."

"Okay, if you're awake now, I will bring you something for supper."

Nurgul nodded. This was really confusing. The woman was Chinese, probably a prison guard, because this little cubbyhole could be nothing else but a prison cell. Maybe she had fainted during the endless questioning and water buckets and had then been brought here. But if it was already supper time, how long had she slept?

Again, the lock creaked and the woman came in with a tray.

"Well, there's not much left but I guess you will be hungry."

"Thank you."

"Did you have a good sleep?"

Nurgul shrugged her shoulders. She did not know. Maybe she had not slept at all, but had been unconscious. She didn't feel well-rested, more as if she had been martyred. But a sip of water was good and she took the tray with some bread and rice soup.

"I'll be back tomorrow morning and get the tray," the woman smiled at her reassuringly. "Good night, number 88. Sleep peacefully, that will be good for you."

Why was this Chinese woman so friendly and why did she talk all the time about a number 88?

"This is your prisoner number. You are prisoner no. 88. We do not have many female prisoners, you know, with men the numbers are much higher."

"Oh, so here I am not Nurgul Mammat but no. 88."

"This is a good sign," the prison guard said cheerfully, "because eight is a Chinese lucky number and a double eight surely brings much luck."

Well, it was not really luck, but now she had at least something to eat and drink, and no one tormented her with questions any more.

On the seventh day a man came from Beijing.

"We have put you in a single cell," he explained, "so that you could not talk to anyone about what you saw. You must never talk about it, do you understand me? Never speak to anyone about it, not even to your husband. And especially not with your sister in Sweden. Don't tell anyone about it. Just forget everything. If you promise to do so, we will release you."

This stranger was much friendlier than the men who had interrogated her, although he was also Chinese. Maybe it was because of his rank? He seemed to be a high official whom the others regarded with great respect. Nurgul had pondered a lot during the last week. Actually, she did not want to think of anything anymore and it would not have been necessary to tell her to forget everything that had happened. Forget it forever and for all eternity. But nonetheless she had asked herself over and over again, *why* it had happened. Why were people shot? No one should kill another human being. Had the dead done anything wrong? Had they attacked the police station? But why was there so much aggression? Why couldn't everybody live peacefully together, whether they were Chinese or Uyghur, Muslims, Buddhists or atheists, officials or farmers? Couldn't they just respect each other? And why had the men always asked the same stupid questions for days on end, tormenting her, even though she had nothing to do with it? She knew that her son had an answer to all her questions, but this was an answer which she did not want to hear. She just wanted to forget.

Nurgul was no longer the happy, even-tempered woman who loved the contemplative life in her village. She had become silent and frightened, wincing at every loud noise and rarely left the house.

When someone asked where she had been during all that week, she said, "At the hospital." When her sister called, she said she could not speak because she had a sore throat. They had given her a medication in hospital, but it did not help. When Barat asked how he could help her, she said, "I'm fine." When the children came to visit, she cooked and baked as she had always done, but her smile had gone. Her happy laughter had disappeared. She had buried all memories of those terrible days in jail deep in her soul. She had built an invisible wall around her and become anxious and silent – much more silent than a woman in a silent Uyghur village should be.

Rozihan

ozihan heard voices outside, and the large yard gate crea-ked in its hinges, as the heavy wings were opened. The gate was already very old, but it was one of the most beautiful yard gates on the street, decorated with intricate carvings and painted in different shades of blue. It seemed that Metkurban had let someone in, because the voices grew louder and the footsteps came closer.

Rozihan was sick. She lay on the supa, which was covered with thick felt carpets, and under the warmest blanket they had. She had slept a restless sleep. Her heart had given her some problems in the morning. She had been close to fainting, but her family hoped she would be better soon. The three girls sat with their grandmother on the other side of the room, listening to the gentle voice singing old songs and rhymes.

They were all startled when they heard heavy, manly steps coming up to the house. Metkurban pushed aside the curtain and two strangers entered the room.

"Rozihan Menssur?" the elder of them said. "We have to take you with us."

Rozihan sat up and looked at her husband and the two men, confused.

"We will take you to Nurluq Hospital."

"Oh, it'll be all right," she replied uncertainly. "It was just a weakness, a little weakness. Tomorrow I will be better."

Metkurban got nervous, he wanted to say something, but the man from the district government was the first to speak, "An abortion will be done."

Rozihan stared at him in disbelief. She was at a loss for words and her eyes began to wander from one to the other, without finding a halt, not even a spark of security. Metkurban seemed to have fallen into a state of shock. She searched his eyes, but they were not there. His eyes were blank. His face had lost all expression. It was only after an eternity, with a sudden jerk of determination, that he found back to reality and said, "No!"

The two strangers looked at him with a disapproving gaze.

"We have received instructions from the district government to bring your wife to the hospital. You have already three children and this is more than allowed."

"No!"

"That is the law."

"No, that's not right. We are Uyghurs and here in the countryside, we are allowed by law to have three children."

"But not four."

"Our three children are girls. We need a boy who can take over the farm one day."

"That is not the law."

"But it is the reality!"

"Do not try to find useless excuses! Rozihan, get ready now, we have to go!"

Rozihan was lying, crooked, on her mat, and wept silently into the pillow.

The three girls crawled into the lap of their grandmother and watched the strange men with anxious faces. None of them moved.

"My wife feels very ill," Metkurban tried to explain. "She had some trouble with her heart this morning. It was not the first time. Her heart is weak and she must be very careful, the doctor said. You must not take her now. Please! She would not survive an operation."

The two men looked at each other.

"Well," the older of the two men decided after a moment, "let her have some rest. Come on, Ablikim, let's go to the neighbor village and pick up the other woman."

Without saying anything more they left the house.

For a moment there was dead silence in the room. The whole family felt paralyzed. It was as if they had received a blow to the head or as if a black sand storm had enveloped them in deadly darkness. Rozihan stopped crying. Metkurban stood frozen next to her bed and none of the children dared to move or to ask a question. But they knew that something terrible had just happened.

"They will come back, Metkurban."

"Maybe. Maybe not. Maybe they will leave us alone, because of your heart problems."

"Go!" a voice came from the corner of the room where Metkurban's mother was sitting with her granddaughters. "You have to hide until an abortion is no longer possible."

"We cannot leave you alone with the children and father. Father is sick and needs care. Nigare is old enough to help a little, but the twins are still very small. You cannot do it all by yourself. And the farm, the animals... This is impossible, Mother. Moreover, sometimes they do an abortion even in the eighth month, I've heard. No, it does not make sense. Anyway, where should we go?"

"Mahire, a woman from the neighborhood, told me that one of her nieces had hidden in the house of some relatives in another village until the child was born. And then no one could kill it."

"Let's wait until tomorrow, Mother. Rozihan is far too weak today. If she had to travel for hours on a donkey cart, the child would be lost anyway... and maybe she will be as well."

Rozihan was six months pregnant. Though she was already thirty-six, the pregnancy was easy. Only her heart had some problems. Perhaps an operation could help, but surgery was not an option because it was much too expensive, and the doctor had said that it was not too serious. If she were careful and did not work too hard, she could live with her heart until she was hundred years old.

Of course Rozihan and Metkurban knew that according to the law they were allowed to have only three children, but a rumor was going around that families in the countryside had the right to have a son. There were more than enough examples, and they had never heard of anybody having difficulties because of it. Metkurban had always wanted a son, not only because it was the pride of every father to have a son, but also for a very practical reason. He was a farmer. He had a few fields planted with corn and wheat, a cow, some chickens and sheep. His father had witnessed the Mao era when all land had been organized into communes and when all farmers had to toil under the relentless supervision of party officials. He had not been allowed to take a single ear of corn, matured in a field that once had belonged to his family, because everything belonged to the commune, and was divided or sold as the party leaders thought was right. Often the families had to starve, even though the country was fertile and although they worked harder than ever before. Later, when Mao died and the Cultural Revolution was over, the peasants were given back parts of their former land. Though the land still belonged to the state, the farmers could cultivate the fields as they wanted. That was why Metkurban needed a son who could help him and, when he was old, take over the farm. The girls would get married and live with their new families.

From time to time, one heard about a girl that had died a few hours after birth, and often people suspected that this was not a sad blow, but that the parents had wanted to keep open the option of a new pregnancy. For Rozihan and Metkurban this was unthinkable. Their little daughters were a precious treasure to them and so they had had faith in Allah and left the decision to him whether he would give them a son or not.

Rozihan caressed her belly. She felt a lump under her hands that slipped away and reappeared elsewhere. Was it a foot? Or the head? In any case, it was her child and it was alive. It would come in a few months and it wanted to grow up with the three girls and live a happy life. Maybe it was the son that Metkurban wished so much to have.

Again there was silence in the house. They all had the feeling that talking about their fear would aggravate the situation. The only sound to be heard was a low moaning coming from outside, from the porch next to the entrance. Metkurban hurried out. At noon, they had bedded his father there so that he could breathe more freely in the fresh air. The father was suffering from a serious illness and was dependent on the care of his daughter-in-law. He had not understood why the two men had come, but now, as it was so unusually quiet in the house, he felt a vague uneasiness rising inside him.

"It's nothing, father," Metkurban calmed him. "They have looked after Rozihan and asked if she needed a doctor."

"She should rest. Make sure, Metkurban, that she takes a rest. We want her to give birth to a healthy, strong boy, don't we?"

Ablikim smiled contentedly and sank back on his pillow. Yes, he wanted a boy in the family, a grandson, who would one day take over the land that had belonged to his forefathers. His father and grandfather had once told him about the time when they had cultivated their fields in the way it had been done for ages in the oasis, with their own hands, and in harmony with nature. With horror he thought back to the time of his own youth, when all the land belonged to the people's communes, and all farmers had to obey ignorant party officials, and were debased to simple farm workers with no rights. So many senseless rules! So much suffering! The men had to live away from their families in bunkhouses. They had to take their meals in the village canteen. They had to run to the fields, back to the canteen, to political meetings, to dinner, to the barracks, and wasted so much time by running from one point to the other instead of working in the fields. Therefore the crops were bad, not good, as the party officials invariably proclaimed. Every year they praised the successful harvest and ensured that the target figures were met, even exceeded. Ridiculous, the peasants had thought in secret. You cannot subjugate nature by planned targets and political dictates. You have to listen to nature, love it, and learn from centuries of experience. You have to accept that you live in a desert region where rain is rare. You have to treat water as a precious resource. Of course, one can drill wells deeper and deeper into the soil and pump groundwater, but would the groundwater be sufficient forever?

The waste of water had not ceased with the end of the Cultural Revolution, Ablikim thought. Now there were enormous cotton plantations, managed by Han Chinese who strived for profit and pushed for bigger and bigger crops on the back of nature. Cotton needs huge amounts of water. The farmers knew that and had planted wheat and corn. But now the Chinese wanted to have cotton that they could sell to the textile industry or abroad. It destroys our land, Ablikim mused. *Our* land.

Tired, Ablikim closed his eyes. I am so happy that I have a good son who understands the land, he consoled himself, and soon I will have a grandson, too. Everything will be all right. And then he dozed off, happy.

That night, only the children could sleep. The adults were restless under their blankets, each of them caught in their own sorrows and fears.

Rozihan could not sleep because she was tormented by a terrible fear. She had heard of forced abortions, though not in the district of Keriya. But some women told stories that had happened somewhere in China, for the one-child policy concerned not only Uyghurs, but also everyone else in the People's Republic. But here in the countryside, near the Taklamakan Desert, no one had seriously expected such strict measures. Her two younger girls were twins, so she had been pregnant only twice and therefore, she argued to herself, the government should give her the chance to have a son. Would the men come back?

They had said that they would pick up another woman from a neighboring village. Maybe the regulations will be controlled more strictly in the district of Hotan? She tried not to think about it, but the fear remained. She put her hands on her belly and comforted the little creature that was stirring inside. I will protect you as well as I can, darling, she promised. But I do not know if I really can. The government and the Party's rules are stronger than me. They can do whatever they want. Tears flooded her cheeks and she tried to suppress a loud sob.

Metkurban thought, "Why do men do such things? They are Uyghurs like us, but they want to take our child. Why do they work for a government that is dominated by Han Chinese? In Beijing they make laws and impose them to us. Even here in our country which is called the 'Autonomous Region,' we have no right of self-determination. It's always the Chinese who have the final say, and we are their henchmen. But why? Why do some people work for a government that does not care for our people but only for power and profit?" Metkurban rolled to the other side and hit with his knee against the small table he had forgotten to clear away. "Heck," he thought. "It's all bullshit! They ruin everything! Our country, our culture, our traditions! And now they even come to take away our child. What has happened to our people? We should stick together and protect our identity." Angrily, Metkurban rolled back to the other side and saw that his wife was crying. He put his arm around her, but had no comforting words.

Metkurban's mother thought, "How can people think of such a thing? Every child is a gift from Allah and no one has the right to kill it. Not even in the womb. This is cruel. This is a law against nature. And Rozihan is almost seven months pregnant, the child is not a tiny fetus anymore, but a real little child with all its limbs and senses and everything it needs to live. This is cruel. Perhaps it is also dangerous for the mother. What would we do without Rozihan? The children, my husband, the fields... Maybe in the huge cities in China's east there is not enough space and food for more and more children, but here we need them. We farmers can feed our children and they have plenty of room to play. A farmer needs a son and our nation needs children.

Metkurban's father did not sleep either. Since his son had taken him into the house before dinner, he felt that something was wrong. In the afternoon on the porch, he felt comfortable and happy that he was to see his grandson and heir soon. That would give him new strength and then he would be able to rise again and help Metkurban with some easy work. His son had so much to do, since he himself was bedridden. Were they trying to conceal something from him? Maybe it had to do with the two men who had been here in the afternoon? Ablikim had the feeling that an invisible threat was hovering over the house, and he was very worried.

The sun was shining, the sky was blue, and if the air had not been so misty in the far distance, one could have seen the high mountains of the Kunlun Mountains. Unfortunately, mist or dust often obstructed the view of these snowy giants, behind which lay Tibet. Metkurban loved to see the white snow on the highest of the mountains, the "Goddess of Kunlun," against a deep blue sky. But today probably not even this goddess could have improved his mood. He felt terrible after a sleepless night, tormented by rage and concern.

It was just like every morning. Nigare and her grandmother tidied up the beds and laid the breakfast table. The two little girls jumped happily around in the yard, and Rozihan prepared the food. She got out of bed, although she still felt weak, but her heart had calmed down and she did not want to leave all the work to her mother-in-law.

"Apa, Apa!" The twins came breathlessly into the kitchen. "Apa, I'm hungry!"

"I'm hungry," chirped the sister as she bounced on one leg around her mother.

"What are you cooking?"

"Corn soup and lamb with potatoes."

"Mmm, corn soup."

"Mmm, potatoes," both chattered happily.

"It will take a moment, children. Go look if grandpa is ready."

The two little girls ran out into the yard to meet their father and grandfather coming back from the toilet.

"Hello, my little princesses," Metkurban smiled, although he did not feel like smiling. When seeing these two beautiful, healthy little human beings, all the thoughts that had tormented him all night came back and anguished his soul. "Are you already waiting for breakfast?"

"Yeah!" they cheered in unison. "Come on, Grandpa. Come on, I'll help you."

One of the girls took the old man's hand and ran a few steps ahead of him.

"Wait, my little one, I am not as fast as that. I need the strong arm of your father."

When the family had almost finished breakfast, they heard a car stopping in front of the gate. A car door slammed, then another one. Someone called in a commanding voice, then knocked at the gate.

Rozihan felt her heart shatter. Metkurban winced and remained seated, as if a sudden flash of lightning had taken all the power of his life. His mother stared in horror at her husband and Ablikim looked confused from one to another and said, "Do you know who is coming?"

They looked at him helplessly.

"Who is it? What's going on?" Ablikim was seized by anxiety. "Metkurban, what are you hiding from me?"

There was another knock. Demanding.

"Answer!" The old man got angry with worry.

Metkurban gave no answer but stood up and shuffled across the court like an old man.

"Open the door!" Two impatient fists hammered against the big beautiful gate.

Metkurban pushed the bar and pulled open one wing of the heavy wooden door.

The two men who had come yesterday entered and said to Rozihan, "Rozihan Menssur, pack up a few things and come with us. We will take you to the Nurluq Hospital."

"I can't..."

"You can't take her..."

"What is...?"

"You know why we have to take you with us. Don't try to find excuses!" The older man cut off all objections. "We just do what we have to do."

"But my wife..."

"You know the law!"

"Then I'll go with her!"

The two men exchanged a look. They did not know any orders which forbade a husband to accompany his wife. Therefore they were silent when Metkurban took Rozihan's arm and walked to the door with her. They heard the old man grumbling behind them. Then the men pushed the pregnant woman into the car and off they went over the bumpy dirt road, then a shady, tree-lined avenue, and finally over the dusty highway to Keriya.

The car stopped in front of the hospital. The men led Rozihan to a doctor's room and left. They had done their job. Metkurban was told to sit down in the hallway and wait. He waited a long time. He hoped to be allowed to speak with the doctor and maybe to convince him that an abortion after six months of pregnancy was too dangerous for the heart of a sick woman. Or he could offer to pay a penalty, even though he knew quite well that he did not possess enough money for that, but he could try. Twice he had knocked on the door and asked to be let in, but had been rejected each time. Now the door opened and Rozihan came out with a nurse.

"We will bring your wife to her bed now. If you want, you can wait there, or you can go back home because it does not make much sense to wait. It will take at least twenty-four hours."

"What takes at least twenty-four hours?" Metkurban stared at the nurse. "What are you doing with her? Do you really want to say that an abortion will be done! The child is already big. My wife is sick! You cannot do it! For heaven's sake, Rozihan, what are they doing to you!"

His voice broke down, tears of anger and grief came out and with a desperate leap he took his wife by the arm and pulled her away.

"Come, come quickly, we can run away!"

"Nobody is running away!" a commanding voice thundered. The doctor had risen from his seat and rushed to the door. "Sister Bahar, take this woman immediately to the delivery room! And you," he turned to the husband, "if you want to stay here, then you behave quietly and comfort your wife when her hard time comes."

And before he closed the door, he added, "If I hear the slightest peep, you'll run away indeed. But alone! Got that?"

Metkurban followed the two women, helpless and depressed. Rozihan is like a sheep brought to the livestock market, he thought. Or like a sheep to be shorn. No, that's not right, because wool grows again. More like a sacrificial sheep that is to be slaughtered at the Feast of the Sacrifice. No, that's not right either, because then it has a purpose. It is a gift to Allah and food for many hungry people. Our child, maybe our son, is sacrificed for nothing. For a law. A law not made by us Uyghurs! For a cruel law from faraway China!

The nurse closed the door and left Metkurban outside like a dog. He felt miserable. He could do nothing. Maybe he could crush the door. He was strong and he felt enough anger in his gut, but he knew that it was useless. They would send him home or to jail. He could knock down the doctor and nurses, but at the end he would be arrested by the police and might never be free again. No, he had no chance to fight for his son any more. He just had to sit and wait.

The nurse helped Rozihan out of her clothes and let her lay down on the bed. She talked the whole time trying to calm her, but her patient could not stop crying. Rozihan had no strength anymore to fight. She knew as well as Metkurban that she was at the mercy of these people. There was a law they had violated and now she had to face the consequences, so the doctor had said. She had told him of the twins and that a farmer needs a son, but the doctor had refused to accept any argument.

"We have our orders," he said. "We do not make these decisions. It is the responsibility of the district government. They have already sent several women to us in recent days. We just do what we are told. I'm sorry."

Rozihan was not sure if he was really sorry. She rather had the impression that he did his job and waited for a quiet evening at home.

The nurse placed a noose around her right hand. "I must tie your hands and feet," she said.

Rozihan was overcome with panic. Tied to the bed, like on a torture rack? What were they doing with her? She tried to scream and pull away her hand, but she could not escape the strong grip. Then the other hand was tied down, then the legs.

"Do not worry, my good woman." The nurse tried to calm her. "It does not hurt. We do this only for your own safety. You really do not need to be afraid. Only a tiny stitch and it's over."

She approached with a syringe and then, indeed, it was over.

Over was the hope to have a son, but not the suffering.

"We'll see after you every couple of hours," the nurse promised, as if this could be a comfort. "Can I let your husband in now?"

74

She did not wait for an answer, because Metkurban had already slipped into the room. He came to his wife, and as if there was still a spark of hope, he asked, "How are you, Rozihan?"

Wearily, she replied, "I'm fine, I do not feel anything, but I think she has killed the baby."

"Tell your wife to relax. This is the best for her."

Metkurban and Rozihan spent hour after hour waiting, helpless, exhausted and desperate.

"What did she say is going to happen now?" Metkurban asked after a while, even though he knew very well what would happen.

"She said it can last all day long."

Metkurban felt anger flare up again. If there is an injection to kill, he thought, then there should be also a way to get the poor thing out of the womb. Must Rozihan stay here, tied to a bed, for twenty-four hours and suffer from emotional and physical pain? He jumped up and ran up and down the room. Could they still flee secretly? Was it already too late?

The nurse came in without knocking on the door.

"Well, how do you feel?" she asked Rozihan. "Is it already beginning?"

"What?"

"The labor."

"So the child will be born now?" Suddenly there was again this senseless glimmer of hope.

"Well, it has to come out somehow." The nurse smiled contemptuously about this stupid woman who had already experienced several births. Even a dead child must come out of the belly.

"Just be patient, it won't be long."

Then she left.

"Rozihan, maybe it will not be as bad as with a real birth," Metkurban said, "because the child is still small. I mean, smaller than our daughters were."

His wife did not answer. She wanted to cry, but she could not cry anymore, because there were no more tears in her. If she could not have her child, because the government did not allow it, then at least she wanted to go home and not lie here for hours. The children might cry for her and the old man needed her help.

At this moment, her whole body clenched, a sharp pain shot through her body, a strangled cry wrung from her throat. She tried to convulse, but her legs were still tied to the bed.

"Get the nurse," she gasped. Metkurban ran into the hallway and yelled for help.

"Well, didn't I tell you?" the nurse said cheerfully. "Now it will be done soon. Now I can untie you, anyway it's too late to run away."

Metkurban sat at his wife's bedside, holding her hand and giving her comfort. When a new contraction came, though, he needed comfort himself. He was tired, helpless, empty. Completely empty. As empty as a dried up river bed in the desert, a fountain without water.

A story without words, a song without tones.

Hours passed. One after the other. A birth is always hard for a woman, Metkurban said to himself. For a man, too, because he cannot really help and must see his wife suffer. But after a certain time the suffering is over, and when the newborn cries the first cry, everything is forgotten. Then you have a child as a reward for all the suffering. But this time there will be no reward.

Sometime during the night, he had not been able to support it any more. He had simply not been able to watch his wife suffering. It was much worse than the former births. The contractions were just as violent, the pain was unbearable, and it did not last twenty-four hours but much longer. The dead child could not help like a living child who pushes forward to see the light of day.

76

In the early morning hours Metkurban had left the room. His wife had cried without stopping until she had no voice. She had no longer perceived his presence, had shaken off his hand as if it was an additional torment. She had repelled everything, had kicked with her arms and legs. She had not been in control of herself. She was in hell. Hell cannot be worse than that, Merkurban thought.

A doctor had come and gone. A midwife had looked after her and had gone again. Rozihan had to endure the pain all by herself.

"How could a government allow this to happen?" Metkurban wondered for the millionth time, as he sat in a dark corner of the hospital corridor, covering his ears so that he did not hear the screams. If it was really true that the birth rate had to be regulated by law in order to prevent an over-population, and if it was really impossible to make an exception, then one would have at least to ensure that an abortion was done in early pregnancy and not when the child was almost viable. What Rozihan was going through now was worse than execution. Better a bullet in the head than these endless hours of excruciating pain!

It took more than thirty hours before the dead child was born. The doctor had not come again. The midwife had taken it away. Metkurban had seen her go away with a bundle under the arm. Now a nurse was in the room and washed the patient. Timidly, Metkurban approached. Rozihan lay motionless on the bed. Her face had no expression, the skin was flabby and pale like the sheet on which she lay, her hair was tangled and sticky. His beautiful woman looked like a corpse, but she lived. At least her heart had been strong enough, that was all he was able to think, the rest was mere bitterness. His grief was so deep and staggering that he felt he could do nothing but stand by the bed.

"You can go now," the nurse said casually as she put the washing stuff aside. "As soon as your wife has rested a bit and can stand up, of course."

One week later.

Rohzihan was slow to recover. It took her a lot of time to regain strength, because not only her body was bruised, but also her soul. Her heart had survived the ordeal, but it had suffered an emotional crack which did not heal easily. Maybe it would never heal, but life had to go on. The girls needed her. Metkurban had to take care of the farm. The old man was ill and could barely get out of his bed. Her mother-in-law had her hands full. She was already an old woman and Rozihan did not want to stay in bed for days and let her do all the housework. She knew that she was not the only one in the family who suffered. They all were sad and depressed. Metkurban worked every day to exhaustion in the hot sun trying to forget his feelings and at night he sleeplessly tossed and turned through the darkness.

Once, when he noticed that Rozihan did not sleep either, he said so softly that she could barely hear it, "Did you see it?"

For a long time she did not answer. Then she replied just as softly, "Yes, they put it beside me on the bed. Perhaps as a punishment, I don't know. Maybe they wanted me to see what I've done. It was my own fault, because we did not pay attention... because we had broken the law. Then the midwife took a towel and wrapped it in it and went away without looking at me."

Rozihan felt that Metkurban wanted to know something else, although he did not dare to ask.

"It was a boy." And after a long pause she added, "He had quite a lot of hair."

Nigare came running into the house shouting loudly,

"Dad, please, come. Grandpa is not well."

Metkurban got up and walked out. Ablikim loved to be outdoors, but in the past few days, the fresh air had brought him no relief. The news of the violent death of his grandchild had taken his last strength and the will to live. At first he had not believed it to be true. He had repeatedly said, "The Party does

78

not do such things. It cannot be. I once believed in the ideology of the Party. I know that many things are not right and I know that many officials work more for themselves than for the good of the people, but it cannot let such a cruel thing happen. To kill a child... no!" He did not want to believe it.

Ablikim looked at his son who crouched beside his bed. He wanted to say something, but he had no force. Nigare caressed his wrinkled hand. The two women and the little girls also came and knelt beside the bed of the old man.

"Everything is okay, Father," Metkurban said softly. "Do not worry about us. We will make it. You always taught us that we must take life as it is. Do you remember? Not everything is good, you said, but you have to make the best of it. After each sandstorm comes the sun, after the heat of the day, the cold of the night. Do not worry, father. Do not worry about us."

He touched the old man tenderly on his weathered face with the long white beard.

"But it was not fair!" Ablikim whispered, barely audible.

"Where you go now, Father, there will be no injustice," Metkurban thought, but he did not say it. He just drew his fingers one last time over the dead eyes of his father.

The one-child policy was introduced in China in 1979. The reason was the rapid population growth since the founding of the People's Republic of China, encouraged by Mao, who assumed that many children, that is to say, many workers, lead to big economic growth. Later, however, it was feared that one day there might not be enough room and food for such a large population. Slower population growth could increase the standard of living for the masses. But at that time, officials had not considered what to do about the fact that many young couples would rather have a son than a girl and that many unborn or newborn girls would not be given a chance to live. Furthermore, it had not been considered that someday there would be many young men and very few young women, that each child would be spoiled not only by their parents but also by two pairs of grandparents, or that when these children grew up, there would be only one child to provide for two parents and four grandparents. The national pension scheme does not cover the entire population and in the long run it would be impossible to finance, as there are more and more elderly and fewer young people. According to the Chinese Constitution, children are obliged to care for their parents. The old Confucian tradition also requires helping one's parents selflessly, but who knows how long the old traditions can survive capitalist communism in China.

The original one-child policy provided that a couple living in a town could have only one child; a couple living in the countryside could have two children. At that time, someone who was registered in a town could not move to the countryside, and someone registered in the countryside was registered there forever.

For ethnic minorities, including the Uyghurs, the following regulations applied: a couple who lives in a town may have two children, a couple who lives in the countryside may have three children.

The law was soon amended, allowing a second child if both parents were only children, to avoid the problem of couples without any siblings having to shoulder the whole burden of supporting four parents and potentially eight grandparents. In 2013, another amendment allowed a second child if even one parent is an only child. The law was amended again in 2015 to allow all couples to have two children, and ethnic minorities to have three. Harsh penalties remain in force for couples who exceed these limits and have an "unauthorized" pregnancy.

There have been exceptions to the rule: A couple who is rich enough can, with the payment of a large fine, "buy" the luxury of an additional child. Moreover, in theory, local governments may adapt the administration of the rules to local conditions. There is no a clear rule regarding the latest time a forced abortion can occur.

Abdurahman

t was a Saturday evening in April. A group of men was standing at the road that leads from Kelpin to Yurchi. Motorcycles, ambulances, police officers. A strangely oppressive silence hung over the scene of the accident and none of the men dared to ask what exactly had happened. They spoke in low voices and looked aghast at what lay under a dark cloth on the ground. Kelpin is a small town in the district of Aksu and not many exciting things ever happen here. So this little crowd was unusual.

"A boy," the old man heard someone say.

"On the bike over there," another man said, pointing to a fallen scooter.

"He was still in high school."

"No," said the first, "he dropped out of school, I heard. He comes from Qum'eriq."

"But the other two boys were in high school. I know that for sure."

"What happened? A motorcycle accident?" the old man asked.

The other men turned and looked at him meaningfully.

"Oh yes, these young people and their motorcycles..." muttered the old man.

"It was not an accident!"

"Oh."

Those who had got there earlier began portentously to tell the old man what had happened, each of them giving his own version. For none of them had seen it happen with their own eyes.

Only one person had seen it and he was already in police custody. The boy had cried out loudly when it happened, so that officials had noticed him and taken him away. He also was a student and had been in the same class as Abdurahman. Now he was under arrest.

"He's dead," said a bearded man.

"Who?"

"The boy. They shot him."

"Shot... Shot? Who shot a boy?"

"The police."

The old man took a while to think. He was not quite sure what to think of the situation. There was a broken scooter on the roadside, an ambulance had drove away, policemen had ran back and forth and people stood and talked about a shooting. No, of course, it must have been an accident. The young people always drove too fast with these things. In the old days with donkey carts there were no accidents. Maybe the animals were obstinate now and then, or a wheel broke, but they never went too fast.

"Was he going too fast?"

"He crossed a red light. The police tried to stop him and because he drove on, they followed him and shot at him."

"At the bike?"

"At the three boys. They were three. Two are injured and one is dead."

The old man looked at the others, uncomprehending. Yes, now he understood what had happened, but nevertheless he could not grasp the sense of it. Formerly there had been no traffic lights and no checkpoints in the city, and people did not drive so fast, but now, with all these cars and electric bikes, of course there had to be traffic lights. That was right. And he also thought it was right that everyone had to follow the traffic laws. That was necessary. At a red light one should stop. This is important because otherwise you endanger others. But was it right to shoot someone dead, if he did not? Was it right to kill a man because he had ignored a traffic sign? The old man remained a long time on the road and watched what happened next. The other people left, one after another, someone carried the dead body covered by a dark blanket into a car, the bike was hoisted onto a pickup truck, a policeman sprinkled sand on some parts of the asphalt and then the police car also left. Finally the old man stood alone at the scene of the accident, which was also a crime scene, and mulled for a long time over what he had seen. He wondered what had happened to the world. To a world where boys were shot off their bikes.

The news of the death of the seventeen-year-old Abdurahman Ablimit spread quickly. That same night everyone in Kelpin and the surrounding villages knew that he had been shot dead. No one could say why and how it happened, because Rekip, who possibly witnessed the scene, was in prison, and the two boys who had been sitting behind Abdurahman on the bike were injured and in the hospital. Even a farmer who had been watering his garden near the shooting, and who might have seen the incident, had been arrested. And the other boys who had been on their way home at the same time had hidden at a gas station when seeing the police pursuing a bike. From where they were hiding, it had been impossible to see what had happened.

Everywhere in Kelpin county the news enraged people as never before. More and more often one heard of incidents in which Uyghurs were arrested, abused or even killed by security forces without legal cause. Raids increased. Uyghurs were suspected and accused of small trivialities. The officials always assumed that terrorist or separatist activities were involved. Their job was to protect the security of the state. But this young man, who had met his friends in the bazaar of Kelpin, certainly had nothing to do with politics and not the slightest interest in separatism. He had just gone through a red light.

The next morning, hundreds of people gathered to walk in a protest march to the county government. They wrapped Abdurahman's corpse in a white cloth and carried it on a simple wooden bier. More and more people joined the trek. Relatives, friends, neighbors and other villagers who were sick of the increasing violence in the country walked with them in silence. The protest march grew to nearly five hundred people, more than had ever gathered in this village, and it made the authorities uneasy. With growing concern, they watched as the procession grew longer and longer.

"What do they want?"

"It's because of the boy killed yesterday evening."

"This is a demonstration. We have to stop it!"

The officials and the police were quick to agree that such a protest could not be tolerated. So many people, so many Uyghur men with a doppa on their head, marching in silence along the road. This could mean nothing else but danger, rebellion, terrorism, endangering state security. Something had to be done immediately!

Those who followed the bier, wrapped in tense silence, had many things on their minds. One wept for a friend, a brother, a son; the other mourned for a young man of the neighborhood whom he had seen nearly every day driving down the street on his motor scooter. Many of them still suffered from the shock caused by this cruel, senseless act, and others worried desperately about their sons or friends who had been injured in the shooting and had since disappeared. All were full of sadness and anger. They had come together to demand from the county government a rigorous investigation of the circumstances that had led to the shooting, and for the policeman who had fired the deadly shot be punished according to the law.

At least they wanted to see justice done this time.

The officials, however, did not see in this march a desire for justice but rebellion. Insurrection. These people had to be dispersed at once! Under no circumstances they should be allowed to reach their destination!

Immediately, the police received their instructions. They lined up in front of the funeral procession, forced the men to one side with batons and did not budge. But despite the brutality of the police, the protesters regrouped and when they realized that it was impossible to reach the county government, they turned off and marched towards Yurchi, another village.

The old man had returned to the road after seeing the crowds. He watched them as they passed in silence. He too was now wearing a doppa and he had put on his best long coat, because it was Sunday. According to his religion Friday was the main holiday, but since Sunday was said to be a public holiday, he put on his good coat on both days, Fridays and Sundays, when he went out. He slowly stroked his beard. Deep wrinkles crisscrossed his sunburned face and gave him a look of profound closeness to the land. He had spent all his life in the fields. He had sown, planted and taken the harvest to the bazaar. He had stroked his donkey and guarded his sheep. He had children and grandchildren and he knew that life nowadays was no longer like it had been before. He knew that the old traditions had lost their importance and that modern technology replaced daily work, and he also knew that he could not keep up with all these new things. He knew he was an old man and that the young ones did not need him anymore. He was not sad about that, because such was life. Some are old and others young. He did not lack patience and understanding. One learns a lot when one has seen the world go round for almost ninety years, even if it was only one's own small world. He understood very well that young people loved to race on fast motor scooters on the roads, that now and again they did not pay much attention to the good old traditions, that sometimes they were high-spirited and imprudent. Yes, yes, he himself had been high-spirited once. In secret amusement, he chuckled into his beard. His eyes lit up, filled with blissful memories. Yes, at that time...

"Stop!"

The procession had come to a halt. Several men were running back, holding their head or a wounded arm and screaming in panic to the others,

"Back! They are beating everything to bits!"

"They've blocked the road to Yurchi!"

Like an invisible wave uncertainty, doubt, outrage and anxiety spread among the crowd. At any moment, a smoldering anger could erupt. Undecided, people looked at each other. Some pushed on, others ran back the way they came. In the distance, blue lights could be seen, cries could be heard, screams of rage and despair. The old man looked with incredulous eyes at what was happening in front of him. "What on earth is the meaning of this?" he asked himself in amazement. He walked slowly by the roadside to the head of the funeral procession, but before he reached it, he was pushed back again.

He had not witnessed such a tumult, such disturbing fear, since the days of the Cultural Revolution when young rioters, in their function as Red Guards, had frightened peaceful villagers. That was long ago. Fortunately, a long time ago...

"They took Abdurahman's corpse."

"They've arrested his uncle."

"They struck down Burhanidin."

"They have detained at least a dozen men."

"They have blocked all the roads."

"They have yelled at the boy's mother to stop wailing."

"They are brutes!"

"They are the police," the old man said to himself and went nervously with his tongue around the last tooth he had. Startled, he stopped, because one of the men running back down the road had almost knocked him down.

"Is it true," he asked, "that they took..."

The man did not hear him.

"Is it true that they took the body?" he asked at random into the mass.

"Yes, it's true," someone coming from the head of the procession answered. "Yes, you're dead right it's true! It is incredible!"

Indeed, it is incredible, the old man mumbled. It really is incredible what humans do to other humans. He stood there, at the side of the road, alone, unnoticed by the excited crowd which gradually began to dissipate. He stood there as he had the night before, not understanding what had happened to the world.

A world in which mothers were robbed of their dead sons.

The next day was quiet again. "Everything under control," the government said. But in reality, it was not quiet. The atmosphere remained tense throughout the entire region. In the streets security forces patrolled, police cars drove up and down and announced unequivocally that all further protest would entail serious consequences.

And, above all, the hearts of the villagers were in turmoil. Everyone wanted to know exactly what had happened but no one really knew. Maybe even the officials did not know, but they claimed that a young motorcyclist had run through a red traffic light and a checkpoint. He had ignored all stop commands and had fled at high speed. When a policeman had emitted warning shots into the air, the motorcyclist had attacked him, pounced on him, stolen his gun and threatened him. Consequently the police officer had acted in self-defense.

But Abdurahman had been shot from behind. The doctor could see from the gunshot wounds that the fatal shot had to have come from behind. Moreover, many shots had been fired, at least eighteen cartridges had been found. The three boys who had hidden at the gas station reported the next day that Abdurahman had been followed by seven or eight police officers. How could he have attacked one of them? They supposed that Abdurahman either had lost control of his scooter or had been hit by the fatal bullet while still driving.

In the following days everybody wondered why the boy had not stopped. Had he not seen the red light or had he ignored it on purpose? Had he forgotten his identity papers and tried to avoid a fine? It was known that the family had financial problems because the father had been killed years ago in a work accident and Bakhtigul, the mother, struggled to eke out living for her children. That was the reason why Abdurahman had dropped out of school and begun to earn some money. And, of course, the parents of the two boys who had been taken to hospital or prison were terribly worried about their sons. Nobody gave them information, nobody told them where their sons were and what they were accused of.

Nobody was able to find out what had happened to Abdurahman's body. The authorities refused to give any information. The mother had no grave at which she could pray for her son.

"I have no grave for my son and I can't even give him a funeral ceremony because all our relatives have been detained," Bakhtigul sobbed. In the two weeks after Abdurahman's death more than fifty persons in and around Qum'eriq were arrested. Every day the police came and every day they took someone with them.

The old man sat in front of his house and watched the peaceful village life, but it seemed to him that it was no longer so untroubled and peaceful as it used to be. Something had changed. A shadow or an invisible cloud had settled over the old adobe houses and a strangely oppressive silence crept through the dusty road. The water in the rivulets passing along the rows of poplars lining the road had dried up because it had not rained for a long time. "Our water is scarce," he thought, "Our gardens dry up because the groundwater is diverted to the big fields of state-run farms. In the past we had grapes in front of the house," he remembered, "and in spring the children played under blossoming apricot trees. Everything has become so different..." And then he became tired from the heavy burden of memories.

He could not keep his eyes open. But suddenly he saw again the dark cloth on the street that someone had placed over the body of a dead boy. A thought flashed through his head: "Not only the earth is drying out, but also the hearts of people. This must not be. We must protect our hearts. We must not let them shrivel in these new times in which the only thing that counts is progress and not our old values and traditions. Formerly life was balanced. Then we, the Uyghur farmers, knew how to treat the earth and reap our harvest despite the dry desert climate. We listened to nature and did not ruin it. And we also listened to each other. We Uyghurs always kept together and we all respected each other. Until the Chinese came."

Suddenly a terrible question startled him. He had not asked it before because that night nobody seemed to know the exact details of the incident, but now this question was so frightening that it grabbed his heart in a vice-like grip; he could hardly breathe because he was afraid of the answer. He looked down the street, but there was no one to whom he could put the question. He thoughtfully fondled his beard and lost himself in the lonely memories of a bygone era.

At the time when the Chinese Communist Party took over, many things had changed. They had brought with them unrest, had tried to rearrange everything. Regulations, orders, rules. The peasants were no longer allowed to cultivate their fields as they had done since time immemorial, because all land was absorbed into rural communes led by party functionaries. It had been a bad time and sometimes they had starved. He had to toil together with other men in labor brigades and live in bunkhouses, while his wife and children were sent to do heavy work in the village. Since those days he bore a secret grudge against the Chinese, even contempt, because they did not understand the land. It was the land of his ancestors, but they had in mind nothing but their Party's rules and profit. Already at that time they had begun to destroy nature.

Yes, and then one day the Red Guards had come and spread terror among the peaceful population. They had not been many times in his village, but one could hear terrible stories from the cities. Well, for several decades, policy seemed to have calmed down, but now there were far more Chinese than ever before. They tried to dictate everything: agriculture, industry which polluted the land, the administration, the police... He knew that nowadays many Uyghur men worked for the city administration and the police, because they had to earn their living and could hardly find other jobs. And there it was again, this question...

"Good morning, Grandfather," a voice pulled him out of his thoughts.

He looked up. His neighbor Hashimjan had come and sat down beside him.

"Good morning, Hashimjan."

"How are you? You look tired."

"I am not tired, I am thinking."

"Ah."

Both of them looked for a while at their feet, lost in thought.

"It will be warm today."

"Yes."

"At night, it's still quite cool."

"Yes."

"But summer will come soon."

"Yes."

"Are you okay, Grandfather?"

The old man did not answer. He continued looking at his feet and his neighbor fell silent, too. They sat for a long time side by side in front of the old adobe house, together in their mutual silence. After a while, the old man broke the silence and said,

"Hashimjan."

"Yes?"

"Have you been there?"

"Do you mean the accident... the...?"

"Yes."

"No, I didn't hear anything. But the whole village talks about nothing else."

"What do you know?"

"All men of Abdurahman's family have been arrested."

"Why? What did they do?"

"Nothing."

"Then it is not right that they have been arrested."

"No, of course not. But the officials say that they plotted a demonstration and this is not allowed."

The old man fell silent again. After a long while he said in a low voice,

"I saw the mourning procession. People kept very calm."

"There were too many", Hashimjan replied. "They were afraid. The government is always afraid when many Uyghurs come together. They think that we want to overthrow the whole country. That we plan a putsch, a revolution or something like that. Five hundred peaceful, unarmed Uyghurs and they are afraid that the entire state will go to pieces!"

The man who was younger by two or three decades than the old man had talked himself into a rage and would have said much more about stupidity, fear and injustice, about the power of officials, police and military, but when he looked at his old neighbor's eyes, he stopped abruptly,

"What is the matter, Grandfather?"

He took his arm and gently caressed the bony, tanned hand. It shivered. The old man seemed to suffer a deep inner anguish.

"Hashimjan, I must know it..."

"What, Grandfather?"

The old man hesitated. He suddenly had difficulties asking the question which had oppressed him for several days, because the answer might be even worse than the unanswered question. But nevertheless he had to know the truth. Otherwise he would never be at peace.

"Hashimjan?"

"Yes?"

"The police officer who did the shooting, was he a Uyghur?"

"This is what has disturbed you so much?"

"Yes."

The younger man, still holding the skinny old hand in his hands, patted it gently and, for a moment, he felt overwhelmed by a chaos of compassion and bitterness, emotion and anger. The old man was right. It was a sad truth that so many Uyghurs made themselves henchmen of the Han Chinese. You could not blame them for working together with them. That was only right and proper because Xinjiang was a part of China and nearly half of its population was Chinese. But it could not be right that Uyghurs fought against Uyghurs. It was important for them to participate in the government activities, in the leadership of civil services and all branches of economy and industry – according to the constitution they even should hold the highest positions – but it was not right to hire them to pursue and humiliate their fellow countrymen. There were young guys, so it was said, who did not mind cutting off an old man's beard or tearing a woman's veil from the head if their Chinese superiors told them to do so. Hashimjam needed a moment to master his feelings and continued holding the hand of the old man who had worked a lifetime in sun and cold, in the fields of his ancestors, and who now trembled under the burden of his age and fear for the sake of his people.

"The boys," he began calmly, "the three boys, who had been driving their scooters behind Abdurahman and then had hidden at a gas station, clearly saw in the light of the full moon that all eight policemen pursuing Abdurahman were Han Chinese."

The old man breathed an audible sigh of relief. "Is that true?"

"Yes, none of the policemen was Uyghur."

"I couldn't have borne it..." Embarrassed, he twitched at his beard and muttered some unintelligible words. Then he turned to his neighbor and smiled at him, sad and tired at the same time.

"Thank you, Hashimjan."

And to himself he said, "It is a bad thing to shoot someone to death just because he ignored the call of a policeman. This is bad, this is terribly bad. But if it had been a man of our own people, then my world would have collapsed. We have to stick together. What will become of us, if we tear each other apart?"

Gulmira

amila is absent again," Gulmira heard a classmate whisper to her neighbor. "With all these absences she will never pass the exam."

The two girls sitting behind Gulmira continued whispering in low voices and then began to laugh. This made Gulmira angry, because Ramila was her friend and she knew that she was really sick and did not skip school out of laziness. She also knew that Ramila was often very sad about it, for she wished to become a nurse more than all of the girls in the class. Because her health was weak, she wanted to conquer diseases or at least to learn how to make them more bearable for patients. That was her dream, and although she often felt weak and her body had little strength and endurance, she did everything to get the best grades she could and to fulfill her tasks with diligence and care. Her mental strength remained unbroken and therefore Gulmira admired her friend.

In the first year she had paid little attention to Ramila, because she was so quiet and shy. She was small and frail and so pale, as if she had never been in the sun, but her black, wavy hair caressed her delicate face with big eyes that answered every look with a soft friendliness. Only now in the final year at the nursing school, Gulmira had found a place beside Ramila and they had become close friends.

Gulmira's family usually did not talk about feelings, but with Ramila she could, and that was the reason for their very special friendship. Ramila understood everything that she herself could not explain. She was more familiar with feelings than anyone else, because as a child she had not been able to frolic with other children, she had not been allowed to jump in the warm desert sand or swim in cold streams. Thus, she had lived with her illness and attempted to fathom what was going on in people's souls.

Gulmira was the exact opposite. She was lively and healthy, her round face radiated with joyful warmth, her eyes disappeared almost to slits when she smiled, and she smiled nearly all the time. She did not like her eyes, because they almost looked like Chinese eyes. And besides, she was a bit too thick. But there was no helping it, because she loved to cook and to eat.

Over time, Gulmira and Ramila had become best friends and spent much of their time together. They learned together and shared their dreams. Both wanted to become a nurse and help suffering people; both wanted to find a wonderful man with whom they could fall in love with as soon as possible. Later, they would start a family, but would never lose sight of each other, they swore. They would always confide to each other their secret joys and sorrows. Just like now.

Therefore, it caught Gulmira completely by surprise when she learned this afternoon that Ramila was not just sick, but terminally ill. In the morning, the doctor had spoken openly for the first time and in great detail with Ramila and her parents about the disease. Nobody could say definitely what the cause was, he explained. There was worldwide research that was constantly gaining new insights. Among other things, some research pointed to nuclear radiation as a cause of leukemia, and especially here in this area, it would be conceivable that this was the case, but it could not be scientifically proven, and he advised them not to attach too much weight on this argument because it was a very sensitive issue. Then he talked about the different types of leukemia, its progression and the slim chances of a cure. Although today much more is known about the different conditions, phases, cytostatic drugs, radiation therapy and stem cell transplantation, in Ramila's case none of it was possible because there was no way to do it here, and it would be very expensive.

The conclusion was that Ramila had practically no chance of survival.

How much time did she still have? The doctor could not tell.

Previously, there had never been cases of leukemia in this region on the northern edge of the Taklamakan. Many people said that cancers had been virtually unknown here. The same was true of the frequent birth defects and other inexplicable illnesses and paralysis symptoms. The cancers had to be due to radioactive emissions from the nuclear testing area of Lop Nor. There was no proof, the government would say. The necessary precautions had always been taken and since 1980, only underground tests were performed. But the inhabitants still wondered how the unusually large number of mysterious diseases could be explained, if not by radioactivity. And what precautions had they been! Their villages and towns were only two or three hundred kilometers away from the test area, and they wondered, how far can radioactivity reach? And how long does it last? Not just a few years, as the authorities wanted to make people believe, but thousands, perhaps even millions of years, some people said who knew a lot about these things. Could it really be enough to keep doors and windows closed during the blast, or, if you did not make it home in time, to crouch on the ground and protect your head with both hands? Ordinary people had not given much thought to it, and later, when the test site was no longer used, they went there, climbed over the fence and searched for items that the workers had left behind. Some of it could still be used or sold. In the bazaar, there were buyers for everything and these things still looked good, not dirty, not broken.

But then more and more mysterious diseases appeared, for which the doctors could not find a cause, and at the time nobody except the government doubted a direct correlation between the radiation and the illnesses.

Gulmira was scared to death when she heard the news. She looked at Ramila in disbelief. She saw the familiar, delicate face, the black curls that were braided together in a braid, and the large, dark eyes that had wept.

"That cannot be true, Ramila. There are always new research findings and therapies. We just learned that. Don't you remember? Even cancer can be healed."

"Not this one, it seems."

"You must not give up, Ramila!"

"I think Dr. Wang has done it."

Ramila stared at her clasped hands so that Gulmira could not see the tears that were standing in her eyes. But of course Gulmira knew how she felt and she knew as well as her friend that it was impossible for either of them to hold back their tears. They embraced each other with all their love and wept until there were no more tears left.

"Actually, I wanted to tell you some news. But I don't think I can do it now."

"Why not?"

"It would make you even sadder."

"Nonsense, I love news."

Gulmira hesitated. When she had arrived one hour ago, she was beaming with happiness. She had waited the long school hours to tell her friend about the previous evening, about her incredibly good news, but suddenly, everything was different. Her own happiness seemed to have become meaningless in view of Ramila's misfortune. How could she be happy when Ramila was terminally ill? How could she look forward to a wonderful future while Ramila had no future at all? How could she talk about her first love while Ramila was preparing for death?

"Come on, Gulmira! What happened?"

"I will tell you another time."

"No, please, tell me now. Nothing can make me sadder than I am, and if it is something good you have to tell, it will be like a medicine."

98

"Okay," Gulmira began solemnly and sat down on the bed. She cleared her throat, somewhat embarrassed, and said with a grave look, "Yesterday I was with my uncle, the professor. He had invited some of his students for dinner and he asked me to help with the preparations, together with my cousin Bahar and some other girls."

Salim and his friend Halmurat were invited to dinner with Professor Kasim. A nice little get-together, the professor said, in order to prepare for the upcoming exams.

"We need some help in the kitchen," Professor Kasim greeted his guests, as he opened the door for Salim and Halmurat. "Do any of you guys know how to prepare tugure?"

"Yes, I do," Salim said.

"Very good, here is the kitchen. Let the girls tell you what to do."

Salim went into the kitchen while Halmurat followed the teacher into the guest room and sat down on the pillows that lay around the low table. The table was covered with a high pile of naan, sangza, small cakes, raisins, nuts, fruits and all kinds of colorful candy. In between were some small cups and several teapots.

Salim was quite grateful that he was sent to the kitchen, because there it was more informal than the serious discussions around the table. There were quite a few young people at work. Hamut was stirring in a large pot with noodles that had been pulled to long, thin cords. At a tiny table sat two other girls. One rolled some dough into small round pads and the other one filled these pads with a minced meat filling and folded them to semilunar pockets. Then she called,

"Kamil, is the water boiling? We already have many tugures waiting."

"Okay, bring them here," Kamil answered and said to Salim,

"Hi Salim, it's good that you are here. Do you know Bahar and Gulmira?"

"Hi, essalam aleykum, Bahar and Gulmira. How can I help you?"

"Wealeykum essalam. Do you know how to make tugure?" Gulmira asked, looking at him with curiosity.

Salim sat down at the small table next to the two young women and began to work.

"You're doing fine. Where did you learn that? You're a boy."

"A boy?"

"Well, a man... I thought that men are not able to cook. My father has never been in a kitchen all his life," Gulmira chuckled.

"I like cooking. And I don't think you should generalize: women do this, men do that. Some things they can do together... can't they?"

The two girls looked at each other. Then Gulmira smiled and mumbled,

"Interesting!"

Silently they folded the small thin dough pads for a while and put them side by side on a plate. They worked quickly, Bahar could hardly keep up the rolling and groaned,

"Honestly, together you're much too fast for me. You're a really good team."

Gulmira felt her cheeks flush and, trying to conceal her embarrassment, she asked, "Kamil, are the first tugure ready?"

A little awkward, she got up, took Kamil's plate with steaming tugure and carried it to the guest room.

Salim continued folding the little pads, but he felt very embarrassed and did not dare to meet Bahar's eyes. Why did Gulmira stay away for so long?

"Your name is Salim?" Bahar interrupted his thoughts. "Are you Professor Kasim's student?"

"Yes, I am studying economics. And what do you study?"

Actually, it did not interest him what Bahar studied. The only thing that interested him was when Gulmira would come back and sit near him to fold more dumplings. If it were up to him, it could last the whole night long.

But Gulmira was sitting on a pillow in the guest room, listening to the conversation of the students and thinking, "He is a nice boy, he can cook and is really good-looking. What does he think of me? I wish I could go back to the kitchen, but Uncle Kasim might be angry. He has told me to sit with him." Uneasily, she slipped on her pillow from one side to the other and tried to show interest in the theories of the guests until the plate was empty and she had a reason to leave.

Salim looked up from his work. She smiled. At this instant he lost his heart.

For the rest of the evening, Salim and Gulmira sat together, talking or silent, letting the world go its course, and saw nothing else but two shining eyes. When the professor began to play music and invited the young people to dance, they took each other by the hand and followed the rhythm, without paying attention to the beat of music or their steps. They were no longer present, they were far away in the infinity of feelings.

At the end of the evening, Salim did not know how time had passed, what they had said or done. Only one question interested him,

"May I take you home?"

"Yes, of course," Gulmira replied shyly.

Her parents lived not far on one of the side streets.

"Why do you live so close?"

"It's like that."

"Let's go a little further and then I'll take you back home, okay?"

Salim listened to Gulmira's words. She talked about her family, her schooling and this and that. He listened attentively, but actually he heard only his heart beating so loud that it drowned out everything else. He wanted to know everything about

Gulmira, but in reality, he only wanted to know whether she liked him as much as he liked her.

Before Gulmira left her friend, Ramila said:

"Please, don't tell anybody about my disease. Next week, I will come back to school. I am still alive. Perhaps I still have many years to live, who knows? I really need to finish my studies and hold my diploma in my hands. Even if I won't be able to work as a nurse later on, I absolutely want to complete the training course successfully. That has always been my dream, and if I can't reach at least this one goal, my life would not have had any sense."

"I promise."

"I don't want to be pitied, do you understand? I want to live a normal life as long as possible." And with a roguish wink of the eye she asked,

"Will you see him again?"

Gulmira hugged her friend and held her embrace for a long time.

"I hope so," she whispered. "And what do you think? Will he call me? "

"Of course. Of course, he will! He must! After all, I want to hear the follow-up of the story. "

All of a sudden everything was different. It was as if the world was spinning in a different direction. In the evening, Salim no longer went to the sports ground but went on walks with Gulmira. Basketball and ping-pong hardly interested him anymore. He did not spend his spare time with friends, drinking beer and eating kebabs, but waited for Gulmira. She always came late to appointments. He always came too early. He did nothing but wait. During the day that the evening came, and in the evening that Gulmira came. He knew this was normal, that girls always came late. They have to keep their devotee waiting so that he realizes how difficult it is to win her heart, that she is not easy to have and that a man must be patient if he wants to win her affection.

And when finally she came, they went together to the movies or walked through a park and the dark city streets, and sometimes, casually, their hands touched. A mysterious shiver then spread through their hearts. But in public it would have been bad manners to show that you were in love. That was impossible. You had to behave like casual acquaintances, even if your heart was in flames.

Ramila soon returned to class. Every afternoon, the two girlfriends sat together and while Gulmira talked about her last experiences, Ramila listened enthusiastically and waited impatiently for any continuation of a wonderful love story that she herself would never have. The two girls laughed, made plans and studied for school, until Ramila was too tired and needed to rest.

Months went by. Salim had passed his exams and found a job at a small enterprise, but he had not yet found the courage to confess his love to Gulmira. He did not want to make a mistake. He was afraid to scare her, saying the wrong thing. Even if he knew now how to deal with numbers and finances, he did not know how to behave in these sensitive things of life.

One day they were strolling together in the city park. It was cool, and then dark clouds came up and the first drops fell.

"It's starting to rain," Gulima moaned. "What shall we do?"

"We can buy an umbrella."

They bought a cheap umbrella. It would not last long. It would certainly not survive a thunderstorm, but for the moment it was good enough. The park was now deserted. No children were playing, no strollers were about. They were totally alone and walked silently side by side under their umbrella. They were so close to each other that it was impossible to avoid the occasional accidental touching of their elbows. Salim became restless. How should he hold this stupid thing so that Gulmira did not get wet? Should he put his arm around her shoulder? Or would that be too intrusive? Maybe he could pull her nearer to himself so that the umbrella would protect both of them. After all, the rain water was already running down his back and his jacket was all wet. Or, he could stand still, embrace her tightly and kiss her... she will find me impertinent. She will like it. She will resist, defend herself. No, she will be disappointed if I do not. There is no one here, no one who can see us. She will complain to her parents. Or to her uncle, the professor, and then he will blame me and I will be ashamed for all eternity. But I think she likes me too. Otherwise, why did she look at me that way a while ago? Did I just see it, because I wanted to see it?

"The rain is over, Salim."

Confused, he folded the umbrella and looked at her uncertainly. A look full of expectation. A tender look. Or not? Whether tender or not, he did not have to think about it any longer, because the umbrella had fallen to the ground and as if by magic, his arms had opened and held Gulmira firmly embraced. How did he ever have doubts? They belonged together. It was very simple. Why not listen to one's feelings rather than to thousands of rational and irrational reflections?

Ramila cried. She cried not only because she was happy about Gulmira's happiness, but also because she was sad. She herself would never meet a man like Salim at a party and fall in love or stroll under an umbrella with him. She had come to terms with her fate. She did not hope for miracles, but she had one single wish, an immense wish, and that was to finish her training as a nurse, to have accomplished at least one thing in her life. She did not envy her friend's happiness, but she prayed that she would have enough strength to get through the last weeks leading up to the final exams.

One day, Ramila was missing again from the classroom. She was in the hospital, the teacher said. She suffered from a serious, incurable disease, leukemia.

"She will die," he added.

"She must not die before she has completed her studies," Gulmira said. "It's her biggest dream to have a degree as a registered nurse. Can she make it?"

"Impossible. She might not be able to leave the hospital again."

Gulmira went to see the headmaster and asked if the school could make an exception and issue Ramila's certificate in advance. Nobody doubted that she always earned the best grades and would pass all exams with flying colors, the theoretical as well as the practical ones, if only she had the physical strength to keep up. The headmaster conferred with the council and at the end he presented a diploma with an official seal and all of the signatures.

On one of the following afternoons, Gulmira and some of her classmates went to the hospital.

"How nice of you," Ramila said gratefully. "I am so happy that all of you came."

"How are you?"

"I always feel tired, but I think I'm getting better. I would so much like to come back to class before the exams start. Did I miss much?"

"Not so much. Actually, we've almost finished the school year. It will not be long until our certificates are prepared. Don't worry. We brought something along for you. Because you still have to stay here for a while and because you have best grades in all subjects, yours is ready now. Look here!"

Gulmira took the diploma with signet of the school, all stamps, signatures and Ramila's name written in big letters. She held it high into the air.

"My diploma?"

Tears sprang into her eyes. She stared alternately at the certificate and at the girls who stood around her bed. Half sobbing, half beaming with joy, she stammered,

"Does that mean that I'm now a real nurse? Does that mean that I can work in a hospital as soon as I am healthy?"

"Yes, of course. This is your diploma. Congratulations!"

Ramila lay her head down on the pillow and closed her eyes, exhausted by happiness.

She caressed the precious document with her hands, let it fall on the coverlet and said softly,

"Thank you for bringing it. I was very afraid that the last semester would not be recognized, because I have so often missed school. But now everything is good."

When Ramila seemed to have fallen asleep, the other girls slipped out of the room and left Ramila alone with her happy dream.

For Ramila, her greatest wish had become true. She received her diploma as a professional nurse. She was unable to practice her profession, for she only had a few weeks more to live.

For Gulmira, too, a dream had become true. She had found a man who loved her and with whom she wanted to share a long and happy life.

And China had realized Mao's great dream of having nuclear weapons, ready at any moment for use.

A song

میهمان
ئۇيغۇرخەلق ناخشسى

Guest

I invited a guest to my house
Treating him with great honor
But I was forced to give up my house
Even though I am the real owner

میهمان باشلىدىم ئۆيگە،
ئاستىغاسىلىپ كۆرپە،
ئەمدى مەن كەرەلمىدىم،
ئۆزەم ياسىغان ئۆيگە.

I lost my sweet house
Just for hospitality
Now I live in the desert
Barred from my home and orchard

میهماننى قىلىپ ئەززەت،
ئۆيدىن ئايرىلىپ قالدىم،
باغلاردىن ئورۇن تەگمەي،
چۆلگەكەپىلەرسالدى.

The oasis I made
Is filled with uninvited guests
They took all my harvest
Paying no respect, not a cent in
payment

چۆللەرنى قىلسام بوستان،
مىهمانلارتولۇپ كەتتى،
شبخنى يەرپ قويماي،
مىۆسنى ئېلىپ كەتتى.

I invited a guest to my house
Treating him with great honor
Taking all for granted
He turned himself into my master

مىهمان باشلىدىم ئۆيگە،
ئاستىغاسىلىپ كۆرپە،
ئۆزى تۆرگەچىقىۋلىپ،
بولدى خوجايىن بىزگە.

(Translation by a Uyghur scholar who wishes to remain anonymous)

n the 1980s, after many years of cultural constraint under the Mao regime, when a cautious spirit of optimism, a whiff of freedom emerged in China, the Uyghur singer Kuresh Kusen inspired his public with songs that addressed the very things that were on the minds of all Uyghurs: They had welcomed the Chinese Communists, because they had hoped for peace and justice from the new government, but instead they were despised and pushed aside. They lost their land, their jobs and feared for their culture. Kuresh soon became famous beyond the borders of Xinjiang, he won awards and toured all over the country with his band. However, after all hope of freedom of expression and open-mindedness were crushed on 4 June 1989 by the violent repression of the demonstration on Tiananmen Square, the Ministry of Culture in Urumchi began monitoring every little detail of his concerts. With this song – a song that had long been known to all Uyghurs as a kind of popular Uyghur folk song – his tour through the villages of the Hotan Oasis came to an abrupt end. From then on, all further performances were forbidden.

Kuresh was not able to continue his career as a musician until years later, after he had fled to Turkey, and later to Kazakhstan and Kyrgyzstan. After the foundation of the Shanghai Cooperation Organization, it became too dangerous for him even there, so he applied for asylum in Sweden. With his music, he tried to create awareness in Scandinavia and all over Europe for the Uyghur culture and the plight of the Uyghurs in China. He died in 2006, aged forty-seven, of sudden heart failure.

Since time immemorial, hospitality has been regarded as one of the highest principles in the culture of the Uyghur people, a principle founded on Islam. To violate hospitality is just as unthinkable as abuse on the part of the guest.

Yanar

There where the lake had been, the lake in which he had learned to swim, there was now a row of houses. The creek in which he had played as a boy had become a road. It led to a new group of modern apartment buildings with colorful flowerbeds, which had to be watered day and night so that they did not wither. The river in which he and his friends had built dams, although in spring the water could be so rapid that once it had even swept a bridge away, had become a pitiful rivulet that trickled lost and forlorn in its too-large bed.

Yanar stood on the bridge and looked down into what had once been a river. When the snow in the mountains of Tianshan began to melt, it had driven its roaring, foaming floodwaters downstream and in summer, when the water was not so wild and cold, the children had had fun in its whirlpools or tried to jump from stone to stone.

Now the wide riverbed lay sad and dry below him.

Where had all the water gone? Of course, Yanar knew where it had gone, because it was a problem that everyone was aware of and that got increasingly threatening from year to year. And yet no one did anything about it. They just sat there and watched the old picturesque residential areas of the Uyghurs falling into decay, watched life slowly dying. Slowly and quietly, but relentlessly. A creeping danger that nobody wanted to see, some, because they could do nothing to prevent it, and others, because for them there were more important things to do.

It was more important, for example, to divert the water far ahead of the town and use it for the huge state-owned farms and the new industrial plants that kept cropping up out of nowhere. The fraction of water that remained was needed for the modern city center, for Chinese shopping malls and hotels, for parks with beautiful flowers and exotic trees that needed to be hosed down regularly — otherwise their leaves, covered with dust from the desert, did not get enough sunlight and were therefore unable to produce chlorophyll. And, of course, the neat lawns would dry out if they were not watered daily. But as all big cities in Eastern China had parks with neat lawns, it was impossible for a little desert town in the West to do without, if its party secretary wanted to make the right impression. The water from the mountains had long ceased to meet the demands of today's tremendous progress. It had sufficed for more than two thousand years and had made the Turfan oasis into one of the most fertile places in Xinjiang, maybe even in all of China. It had flowed through the endless underground canals of the ancient Karez system and had guaranteed an adequate water supply for the fields and villages. But now it was not sufficient any longer, and now that the groundwater was being utilized, the groundwater level had in some places dropped as low as two hundred meters beneath the earth's surface.

Yanar went a little further along the road on which, in the old days, he had played with the other children. There was not a person in sight, no bird singing. The old poplar trees were still standing, giving shade, but some of them had already died and gazed with bare, whitish withered branches into the blue sky. Once, he remembered, it had always been full of life here. In summer and in winter, afternoons and evenings, we kids were always outside playing. Heat and cold didn't bother us. And the old people sat in front of their houses and watched or waited for someone to pass by and chat with them for a while. We played and talked. Sometimes an old grandfather told us stories and we children squatted round him listening with fascinated attention. Or in the evening we sat near the tonur when it was still warm from baking bread, and there we dreamed up our own fairy tales and heroic stories.

Where were the people now?

A few years ago, his parents had moved into a small city apartment. Their neighbor, the one who had kept all those animals, had also left because there was not enough water for his livestock and he had been forced to sell or slaughter them all. The neighbors who still lived in the area could no longer grow vegetables or grapes in their gardens as they had done before, and the fruit trees bore no fruit.

That morning, Yanar had been on the other side of the town, where the flat, barren, gray Sai desert sprawled towards the distant mountains, this desert consisting of sand, pebbles and a little soil, where some frugal plants could survive if their roots were long enough to reach the groundwater. If ever it rains, this Sai desert can suddenly turn into a vast green carpet. But now filling stations and shops for excavators and construction machines were strung along the roadside and behind them, as far as the eye could see, there were vast, artificially irrigated cotton plantations. In the far distance, he knew, gigantic steel monsters were churning up the earth searching for new oil deposits or other precious resources which would make far-away China rich and leave the land of the Uyghurs devastated. One day, nothing but the tortured earth will remain, he thought. It had no value, they will say later. It was only desert.

Yanar slowly continued on his way until the road became narrower and gradually petered out in the sand. Before him now lay the dunes, the stunningly beautiful sand dunes of the great desert Taklamakan, with their lightly curved lines, banked up and modeled into constantly new formations by the perpetual wind. He felt light and warm at heart. Worry, sadness and anger dissipated like a soft, transitory cloud that can no longer outlast the steel-blue sky and the dry heat.

Carefully, he stepped on to the sand. He knew how fine and soft it was, as soft as velvet, and much softer than all the sand beaches in the world that he had gotten to know in the past few years. This was *his* desert. Here he had grown up, and although it is the most hostile landscape that you can imagine, because no root finds a hold and no animal food, here he had learned what life is. Because even the desert lives, his uncle had always said, and he, Yanar, he had been able to feel this life. Maybe it was a different kind of life, not the life that can be understood with your mind, but one that only the soul can sense, and maybe only the soul of a child who has grown up on the edge of the desert.

Yanar could feel this life again and he began to climb up the slope of a dune. Step by step. His shoe trampled the furrows, waves and patterns that the wind had charted. A small animal had been here before him and had left delicate tracks across the furrows, waves and patterns. On the other side of the dune, the side facing away from the wind, the surface of the sand was as smooth as a precious, blank sheet of paper on which he could paint pictures. Here, however, the going was difficult because his feet sank deep into the sand.

Nevertheless, he climbed another dune and yet another one, each time a little higher. Right at the top, the ridge was almost as sharp as the blade of a knife. "How is that possible?" Yanar had asked his uncle back then. "Sand consists of many tiny grains, so how can they form such a solid surface?" "Sand has a skin" his uncle had replied and his fingertips had stroked tenderly over the perfectly smooth surface. Yes, Yanar pondered, perhaps sand really does have a skin. Even if you cannot see it.

Time had flown by and the sun was already low over the horizon. It cast long shadows from one dune to the next, so that the elegant, sweeping lines were outlined even more clearly than before. The furrows, waves and patterns were now even more distinct in the sand and Yanar could hardly turn his eyes away from them.

One last time he looked into the distance. On three sides, there was nothing but a sea of dunes, tranquil, peaceful and endless. To the north, behind the city, behind the parks, the new apartment buildings and the shops for construction machines, tiny little drilling rigs towered up like needles piercing the earth.

Lost in thought, Yanar descended the slope. He was worried about his country.

The Sheep

am a sheep. I don't have a name, but my master, that is to say the farmer to whom I belong, is called Abdureni and we live in a small village near the big desert. On our farm, there is a second sheep. My master calls her "the brown one" because her head and legs are brown while I am "the blond one" because not only my wool, but all of me, is blond. I think this is much more beautiful, but to the brown one's mind, I am ugly because my butt is too big. The farmer, however, appreciates it very much because it is the attribute of my special breed. Sheep like me, the fat-tailed sheep, or *Mäkit* sheep as the Uyghurs say, exist nowhere else in China. So, I am a special sheep. Moreover, I have good milk and my meat is very tender and lean and the fat in my tail particularly soft and healthy for people to eat – but this is something I don't want to think about, because I still want to live for many more years. The brown one, for her part, likes to boast of her wool, which is better than mine. Sure, this is good for the farmer, because he can sell it and get some money for it, but I know quite well that he likes me, too. I can see it in his eyes.

Abdureni is already an old man. His furrowed face is full of deep wrinkles and his scraggy grey beard reaches down to his breast. On his head, he always wears a white fabric cap, the *shapaq*, and when he goes out, he puts on top of it a doppa. This is his nice rectangular hat, embroidered in a black and white pattern. Nearly all Uyghur men wear a doppa. Some have them in different colors too, but my master has only this one and I think he looks pretty smart when he wears it.

His wife, the old Amine, always wears a colorful headscarf and a long dress. Sometimes she gives me an affectionate caress when she runs across me, but most of the time she takes care of the chickens and the garden, and of course she has a lot of work to do in the house. She must cook and look after the household. Her children and grandchildren do not live here anymore. They moved into town, but from time to time they come for a visit. And then, I can tell you, hell breaks loose around the farm.

Not long ago, they were here for a few days. The small boy, Abdul, always tried to catch me and wrestle with me. This I don't like. I prefer to be alone and munch my hay or exchange a sheep word with the brown one. I do not like at all these wild games. I always tried to run away but sometimes he caught me and tore my ears or slapped my behind. Then he laughed his head off because I look so funny with my big backside, and knocked me over. Thankfully my master saw it and brought me back to the barn where I was safe.

I like to be in the barn. It is somewhat big for the brown one and me, but formerly there had been more sheep, and anyway it is quite comfortable. The floor is covered with straw which is frequently renewed so that it is always dry and clean. Above our heads there is a loft where the hay is stored for the winter.

Hay has a pretty good taste, but of course fresh grass is better. Whenever Amine has time, she cuts some grass for us from the edge of a field or the side of the road, but now that she is getting older, it is not so easy for her to stoop down. In former times, she had sent the children to cut grass. Now the children are gone and the farmer's back, too, has begun to hurt, he says. So he does not often go out to collect grass for us.

I once was in the mountains some years ago – that was a wonderful time, I can tell you! What an unforgettable experience. A shepherd came from nearby, gathered all the sheep of the village, and led us to the foothills of the Kunlun Mountains where there are real meadows. Endless, vast grassland, all covered by grass and herbs. And the fragrance! You wouldn't believe how wonderful it was! Such beautiful scenery does not exist near our village. Here, most of the time everything is dry and dusty. The desert is near and even after it rains, the grass is scarce.

The farmers depend on deep wells to water their grapes, melons, and orchards. Well, that year we spent the whole summer in the mountains. It was a great time, but at the end I yearned for my master and my barn, and so I didn't mind the long way home. However, it was indeed long and not easy. For many days, we had to cross the flat, vast Sai desert, a very desolate landscape, where there is nothing but dry earth, small stones, and here and there a meager tamarisk bush or another thorny shrub. But we sheep are used to looking everywhere for something to eat and even in that dried-up shrubbery we could find some edible leaves. Of course, they were somewhat dusty, but we are very frugal animals. We do not make a fuss about our food like humans sometimes do.

Did you ever experience a sandstorm? No? Fortunately, at the time we were in the desert, there was no sandstorm, for this could have been tremendously dangerous. There is no place where you can take shelter, only some small bushes – nothing else as far as you can see. But we were lucky – there was no sandstorm. Actually, I am sure that shepherds know a lot about weather and all those things, and they would never take irresponsible risks. When at last we arrived home – at that time we were six sheep on the farm – we were all very happy to be again in our warm and clean barn. The nights had begun to cool down during the end of our tour and later, in winter, even our thick wool would not be thick enough for us to survive outside.

That's how it is, when you are a sheep.

And do you know what else is good when you have a real home and live in a barn? We have our regular meals, not only grass and hay, but also kitchen scraps. Amine is a good cook and when she prepares meals, she gathers all the remains and puts it into our trough. This is good and healthy food for us, and so I don't miss those trips to the fertile mountain grassland. From time to time we even have melon skin. That is something I like very much. Amine cuts it into small pieces and sprinkles

116

it with some wheat husk so that it looks like a super delicious meal. Each time we have melon husk, I sleep like a log and see fragrant meadows and fertile fields in my dreams.

Unfortunately, my master's fields are not fertile any more. They are dry. Nowadays the canals bring little water and the wells are not deep enough. The groundwater level is constantly sinking. Even if the crop is still sufficient for Abdureni and Amine, they have nothing left to sell at the bazaar and that is why they are often sad and worried. Yesterday evening, a neighbor came. He and my master, sitting on the bench in front of our barn, had a long talk, and it was clear they were extremely worried. In a short time, there will not be sufficient water for the animals, though we sheep are very unassuming. But with no water at all, of course, even we can't survive. My master said that he will have to sell his last remaining sheep.

"It makes no sense anymore," he said to the neighbor, and the neighbor answered,

"Yes, I know. It is hard, but you have no choice."

After that, they were silent for a very long time.

"I will go tomorrow morning," my master decided, and the other man said,

"Do that."

Then they were silent again.

"It hurts."

"I know. It hurt me, too."

Once more they stopped talking.

The brown one and I looked at each other. What will happen to us, if we can't stay here in our barn? I have lived on this farm all my life. My master and his wife have always been good to me. They were so proud when I was born, because I was a strong and healthy lamb, and I love them. I want to stay with them for the rest of my life. Who knows how other masters are? I am sure that not all of them are as good and friendly as these two old people. Or they might have little children who want to bop around with me and prick my fat tail. And above all, I don't want to be bought by somebody who is a sheep slaughterer. That would be terrible! I am not a lamb anymore, but I am not old either, and want to live on for many years.

When it grew dark, the neighbor said,

"Well."

"It must be."

"Yes."

"In the old times, we had enough water for all our animals."

"In the old times, we had a cow. Do you remember?"

"Sure. We also had one. Her name was Adile. Every time I called Adile, Amine came and asked what I wanted," Abdureni chuckled into his beard. "And the children were sent to collect the cow droppings."

"It was good fuel, wasn't it?"

"Today we have to buy timber or coal, which costs a lot of money. Formerly our cows provided for the fire in the stove."

"Formerly everything was easier."

"Our children had great fun throwing the cow droppings against the shed wall, where it could dry out."

"Yes, so did my children", the neighbor remembered.

"When the dung was dry, we stockpiled it and whenever Amine needed some in the kitchen, she took it from the shed."

"Yes, yes, that was a good thing."

For a while the two men seemed to be lost in thought. It was completely silent outside. I don't remember the cow Adile. Perhaps she had been sold before I was born, because Amine did not need much milk anymore, since the children and grandchildren moved away.

"Will you go with me to the livestock market tomorrow?"

"I go there every week."

"Sure. There is always something to see."

"You hear a lot of news there. All village men go to the livestock market, whether they want to buy or sell or just look around."

"I will go with my sheep," Abdureni sighed sadly.

"Well. See you tomorrow."

"Good night."

That night, the brown one and I, we slept badly.

This morning we will go to the livestock market. I know that my master and his wife had quite often thought about selling me and the brown one. It must have been a hard decision for them because they are very fond of us and because they had sheep all their life, but now water is so scarce that they can hardly find enough hay for us, and buying hay on the market is expensive. Sometimes they even have to buy vegetables for themselves, because the garden is so dry that the plants wither. I can see that the two old people are worried and I feel sad for them, but I am also worried about myself. To tell the truth: I am terribly troubled.

It is still early in the morning. The sun is shining and not a single cloud is to be seen in the clear blue sky. Summer is like this in our country. It hardly ever rains and the soil dries out if you don't have enough water for irrigation. As the big state-owned cotton plantations outside the villages need enormous quantities of water, there is little left for the small farmers in the oases. That's why they have become poor. That's why we have to go to the livestock market and will be sold.

Abdureni wears his doppa and a grey jacket over the white linen shirt. He enters the barn and puts a rope around our neck. He is talking all the time with us in a low and comforting tone. Well, actually he is talking to himself, I think, because he looks quite low and depressed.

Amine does not accompany us to the bazaar. Probably she does not want to see her sheep led away by strangers. And so only the brown one and I leave the farm with our master and move along the long road to the village, where once a week the livestock market is held.

When we approach the village, we meet quite a lot of people. Some say hello to my master and eye us with an expert look. I begin to understand that today we are not animals but trading goods. Today the main thing is not our well-being but the price we realize. Oh, that hurts! I glance at the brown one who is walking at our master's other side. She trudges along with her head hanging down and apparently thinking of nothing. But that's her way, and after all, you can't blame her for not being a smart sheep like me. On the contrary, I feel pity for the brown one because our master will get much more money for me than for her, as I am of such a special race.

Finally we arrive at some place where we are tied to a wooden pole. All around are sheep, much more than I can count – well, to tell the truth, I don't know at all how to count – but I can see that there are many, many sheep. There are dark and blond ones, thick and thin ones. Abdureni is talking with some men. He looks very serious, sometimes excited, sometimes sad, sometimes angry. Of course, he has to negotiate hard. Everybody does. The men talk and bargain, talk and laugh or grumble, talk again, and eventually one of them takes a bundle of banknotes out of his pocket and hands it over to the seller. Then many other men rush near, gather around and watch the seller counting the notes and putting them in his own pocket. After that, the seller and the buyer shake hands, the spectators nodding their heads and giving more or less wise comments.

Most of the men gather around the big groups of sheep. As we are only two, it is somewhat quiet at our place and Abdureni is sitting on the ground and waiting, when the neighbor from yesterday evening comes by and asks,

""Hi. How is it going?"

"Well..."

"Pretty nice animals."

"Yes, they are good animals. I don't like to give them away."

"I understand, neighbor. When I had to sell my last animals, my heart bled, too. But there was no better way."

The two men are scratching with their feet in the sand.

"They would have died of thirst."

"Yes, there is not enough water. It is not like before."

"Nothing is like before." And after a while he continues, "Nothing is like before! Luckily we live here in our little village far away from the big cities, with all the big politics there. Believe me, Abdureni, my son told me things.... No, I don't understand all these things anymore."

"Me too. I heard about many bad things."

"Are you selling this one?" they are suddenly interrupted. "How much?"

I feel dizzy. A stranger is looking at me with a professional, exacting eye. His fingers rifle through my wool, paw my ears, and finger my beautiful fat tail.

"A little too thin, isn't she?"

What incredible impertinence!

"A wonderful animal," the neighbor interjects. "Not a bit too thin. Exactly as she should be. And look here, this... But no, let it be. I would take her on the spot. For such a good price! It's like nothing."

The stranger gives him an angry look and whispers, "I can see it myself! But please, stop jacking up the price!"

The neighbor steps aside and leaves the stranger and Abdureni alone with their negotiations. I can't look at them and I don't want to hear a single word. They are bargaining for me! Imagine: they are bargaining for the money my master will receive for me. For me, his faithful sheep! I would cry if sheep could cry, but I don't think it's possible. I don't know how to produce tears. But I am as unhappy as never before in my life. If I could speak, I would say to my master that in future I will be content to eat only dusty leaves, that I can do without all the melon skins of the world and that I need only one drop of water a day, but unfortunately I can't speak the human language.

The brown one is watching me curiously. Maybe she begins to understand what is going on. My future and probably her future, too.

I feel sick with anguish and excitement while the two men are talking. Others join them. It seems to be common practice to gather together, building a knot of people, as soon as two men start negotiating. Everybody wants to know what it is about, how high the price will be, who sells his animals and why, if it is a good or a bad deal. All this chitchat must be terribly important for them. Maybe it is a thrilling event in their day-to-day village life.

For me, it is also an important event, but a terrible one. I would never go to a livestock market to see how animals are sold off, because I don't see us as merchandise but as living creatures with their own feelings. But I am only a sheep and I have nothing to decide.

When Abdureni has come to an agreement with the stranger, he unties the rope from the pole and hands it over to him. He caresses my head with tenderness and I have the impression that his hand would cry if it could, but hands cannot cry, just as we sheep cannot cry.

I do not look back while I follow the stranger, my new master.

Perhaps my old master, the cunning neighbor who at least succeeded in making some more yuan in the bargain, and my friend, the brown one, are watching me going away from them, each one with his own thoughts. I myself, I have no thoughts any more. I feel completely empty.

Sad and empty.

Filora

ilora Shukur."

Filora thought she was dreaming when she heard her name.

"Filora gets a prize for her outstanding performance in music... Will you please come on the stage, Filora?"

The girl still did not trust her ears, because she had come to this school only four months ago. She had lived in America for just four months and had not been able to speak a single word of English before that. And now, at the graduation ceremony, she was to receive an award, an award for especially good results! That could not be possible. She thought she heard wrong.

"Filora, please!"

The girl sitting next to her gave her a push with her elbow. Filora got up, brushed back her long black hair and stepped forward. She plucked up her courage, climbed the steps to the stage, and looked at the headmaster boldly as he held out his hand.

"Congratulations, Filora! You have only been with us for a short time, but you have quickly familiarized yourself with the new school system and caught up with stunning success. We all warmly congratulate you and wish you luck and success for the future."

Parents applauded and Filora, a little embarrassed, returned to her seat.

Somewhere in the crowd, somewhere between the parents and relatives of all these pupils receiving their admission to junior high school, sat a small, dark-haired woman, crying tears into her handkerchief. Tears which she could not stop flowing. She was so proud of her daughter! She was so happy. But she had to think back to the long time, to all those many years during which she had left her little girl alone.

Filora had been only six years old when she, Minawar, had had to leave her homeland China. At that time, she had tried to help her brother, who had fled for political reasons to Kazakhstan. She had done her best, had fought with the Kazakh authorities' corruption, lack of understanding, and fanaticism. There had been problems, entanglements, monstrosities, and at the end, she had not seen any way out but to ask the office of the UN High Commissioner for Refugees for help. She eventually received asylum in America. Her husband succeeded shortly after that to emigrate with their small son to Sweden, but Filora had to remain with her grandmother and aunt in Kucha, because the authorities would not issue a passport for her.

Therefore, she went to a Chinese-language Uyghur school for five years.

Filora's thoughts went back to that school, as she sat again in her seat.

Because in Urumchi the majority of residents are Han Chinese, there had been five Chinese classes for each grade and only one Uyghur class. Actually, as a little child, Filora had first attended an elementary school in Kucha, an old town between the high Tianshan Mountains and the Taklamakan Desert, but she hardly remembered that time. The years in Urumchi, however, she remembered very well, and during the last four months she had never stopped wondering about the astounding differences between this school in New York and her old one in distant Xinjiang.

The differences were incredible.

In Urumchi, she had to wear an ugly, scratchy school uniform and the red scarf of the Young Pioneers. Here, students were allowed to wear whatever they wanted.

In Urumchi, three or four Uyghur students had to sit huddled together on a bench. Here, all the students had a chair of their own.

124

In Urumchi, students had to sit upright on their seats, hands on the table, listening attentively and in absolute silence to what the teacher was saying. From time to time, they had to repeat sentences in chorus. Here in America, the students could sit as they wished and the teachers addressed them personally, asked questions, and answered patiently whenever anyone had a question.

In Urumchi, portraits of Mao and the Communist Party leaders hung on the wall. Here, classrooms were decorated with colorful paintings of the students.

In Urumchi, the children had to clean their classroom themselves. Here, they straightened up the classroom, but a cleaning staff mopped the floors.

In some schools in Xinjiang, two students were tasked with heating the stove in the morning and taking away the ashes in the afternoon. Here, the buildings had central heating and no one had to freeze.

In Urumchi, all students had to go home for lunch, no matter how far away their home was. Here, there was a cafeteria and warm meals for everyone.

And the biggest difference of all – and that was why Filora loved America – was the homework. In Urumchi, there was so much homework every day that she didn't have time to play. There were too many times she worked so late at night she was almost too tired to keep her eyes open! But to go to school without having completed your homework, that was... well, that was worse than anything an American child could imagine. That was hell.

Once it had happened to her best friend. Aygul was a quiet, hardworking girl. She always did her tasks with conscientiousness and she never forgot anything. Nearly never, at least. But one day it had happened, not on purpose, of course, not out of laziness or fatigue. That would never have crossed her mind, because the fear of the teacher and her parents would have been

125

unbearable for her. So, she really had always done her best, but one morning she came to school without her mathematics homework, and when she noticed it, it was too late. She had no chance to escape the disaster.

The teacher's face went red with rage.

"Aygul!"

There was dead silence in the classroom. Aygul did not even try to find an excuse. She stood there with arms hanging and her head down, waiting for what was to come.

"I do not know what is going on in your head. How can you compromise the reputation of our school by lacking diligence and discipline?"

What could she respond?

"Answer!"

"I don't know... I just forgot," Aygul stammered. "I am sorry."

"It's too late now! We are all sorry that we have such a careless student like you among us. Shame on you!"

Aygul had tears running down her face, but she did not move. She did not flinch, but let the tears simply drop to the ground.

"Pull yourself together, Aygul! Clean your nose and come here to the podium."

With shaking hands, Filora passed her friend a handkerchief.

"Come here and bring your notebook. Sit down on the floor!"

Aygul did as she was told.

"And now you do your lessons on the floor, in front of the eyes of your fellow students so that they can all see what a worthless, lazy slacker you are."

Filora could hardly follow the lesson. She did not dare to look to the front where a poor humiliated girl, who was her best friend, sat on the dirty floor to solve math problems. This punishment seemed so cruel, ruthless, and unnecessary. Aygul was a diligent student and had forgotten her homework for the very first time in her life. It was not fair! It was mean! In her heart anger, fear and helplessness raged in a hopeless storm of emotions. If the teacher had called on her, she would not have known the answer. Perhaps she would have been punished, too, sent to stand the corner or to write on a piece of paper that she was an inattentive, undisciplined student. Such notes were fixed on the wall so that all could read them. There were many kinds of punishment and they were frequently applied. Maybe it must be like this, Filora had thought at that time, but Aygul's punishment had been too severe. That was for sure.

Filora shook off those memories and let her gaze wander through the festively decorated hall of the American school. Everything was so beautiful, so easy. Never was a child humiliated or beaten. Otherwise, the parents would come and complain to the headmaster.

In America, one had the right to complain. So many things were different here.

But as she was used to working hard, she continued to do so every day since she came to New York. Here, too, she studied at home in the afternoon, but she did it voluntarily. She had to learn English. She *wanted* to learn English so that she could follow the lessons in all subjects. In the beginning, she did not understand a word. She sat in the classroom wondering about her classmates lolling in their seats and snapping their fingers loudly when they knew the answer. There were a handful of black kids, two or three Latinos, and a Chinese girl. The rest were white students. But they all seemed to get along quite well with each other. They laughed together and sometimes even joked with the teacher.

From the beginning, every morning Filora had private lessons in English, so she made quick progress. And after a few weeks, she surpassed the other students in math. What they learned here in the fifth grade, she had already learned in the first or second grade. Even as a little child she had been able to recite the multiplication table by heart. After all, pupils in China were accustomed to learning things by heart – even if they were Uyghur pupils. And since she was also accustomed to endless homework, she did not mind studying late into the evening.

Once, a long time ago, Filora remembered, when she was in first grade, she had to write down the alphabet five times, from beginning to end. The letters of the Uyghur writing are not easy to write for an inexperienced child's hand, because the small bows, curls and points must all be exactly in the right place. You have to be very careful if you want it to look neat. It was late in the evening, almost midnight.

"To bed with you!" her mother had called.

"I'm not quite finished yet." And tears swam in her tired eyes.

"What are you doing up so late? You have to go to school tomorrow morning."

"I have to finish this, Mom, I have to write it all," Filora sobbed desperately. "I have to do it, otherwise Mrs. Mahire will scold me."

"Show it to me."

"It's very bad when we have not done our homework."

"I know, but it's awfully late, dear. You have to go to bed and sleep."

Filora was crying bitterly. She was so tired! She could no longer distinguish these stupid letters. They all looked the same. The many points and curls blurred into a tangled mess before her eyes and tears flowed down on the paper.

"Never mind, I'll do it. Go and clean your teeth!"

The next day Filora could present all five pages with neatly written letters, but the teacher immediately noticed that the last lines were written by another hand. She was upset and Filora felt so ashamed that she wanted to sink into the earth. As punishment, she had to write another five pages of Uyghur letters – in addition to the new homework.

Filora did not like these memories. In China, she had accepted working hard without grumbling, because all children were

128

used to it. But here she loved it and now she even received an award for her diligence!

At the end of the celebration, the audience rose from their seats and sang the national anthem. The young graduates were standing on the stage, a girl in a yellow dress next to a boy in a blue suit, a colorful yellow and blue row, and all of them with a black mortarboard on their heads, beaming, proud and happy.

"Oh, say can you see, by the dawn's early light..."

Filora had memorized the anthem so that she could join in the singing. That had been easy for her, because in China all children learned everything by heart, no matter what text, what formula, whatever. The only thing that counted was to recite it without the faintest deviation. It was more important to not leave out a single word than to understand its meaning.

Qǐlái! Búyuàn zuò núlì de rénmen! – Stand up! All of you who don't want to be slaves any longer!

She had sung the Chinese anthem every Monday morning and every Friday afternoon while she attended the school in Urumchi.

Monday morning, seven o'clock. Time for the great gathering of all students and teachers, for the flag hoisting ceremony, speeches, announcements and propaganda slogans. Sometimes students were honored for outstanding performances. The whole ceremony took about two hours. Two hours of standing and listening attentively, two hours of boredom and absolute discipline. She hardly understood any of the speeches or songs. She was not yet able to understand Chinese well, yet all Uyghur students had to listen during those endless two hours. It was excruciating! Filora still felt bad when she remembered these Monday mornings: all classes had to line up at a fixed place in the schoolyard and only the Uyghur children had to stand directly in the sun where there was not a bit of shade. And since the summer was very hot, even in the morning, this was almost unbearable. They were not allowed to wear hats. They were not allowed to move, to drink, to totter – until a child fell to the ground unconscious. After all, this was something no one could prevent. This happened from time to time, because even Uyghur children are delicate little human beings.

Why did the Chinese classes have the right to stand in the shade and we do not? Filora and her friends asked this question of themselves many times, but they never had the courage to ask it of a teacher, for it never occurred to them that an order could be called into question. This was unthinkable in China.

If an order was not followed, the punishment followed automatically.

For example, when children were late on Monday morning, or when they forgot to tie their red scarf, they had to remain standing outside the gate until the ceremony was over. And after that, not only were the children reprimanded, but also their teachers, and this was really bad for the child, because the reprimanded teachers had to vent their anger.

Give vent to one's feelings...

The future junior high students threw their black mortarboards high up into the air, as high as they could, gaily shouting and cheering. Afterwards, they would all go and celebrate the day with their family.

For Filora there was no family celebration. She just had her mother. Her father and brother were in Sweden, and soon she would go there, too. She would go to a Swedish school and learn Swedish. For the fourth time in her eleven years, she was to learn a new language.

"Do you remember, Mom," she said to her mother on the way home. "Every day in kindergarten we had to learn a Chinese poem before lunch. We Uyghur children just parroted what the teacher said without having any idea what it meant. I just tried to imitate the sound. We got to eat only after at least one child could recite the poem by heart."

130

"I do remember this, dear. You often cried because you did not like to be in kindergarten."

"Yes. It was cruel. Many children cried, because they were hungry and not allowed to eat."

"Your teacher was a Chinese woman. She wanted you to learn Chinese."

"But for the Chinese children, too, it was a torture, sitting there with rumbling tummies and trying to memorize a poem. We were just three or four years old. Imagine if someone here demanded that small children do such a thing!"

For a while they walked in silence through the busy streets of Queens.

"Mom," Filora asked a bit later. "Do you remember my first school in Kucha? I don't have many memories, but I still know that I often felt terribly cold. Why did we have to be outside when it was so cold in winter?"

"Because the schoolhouse was too small. There was only one little room for the Uyghur pupils and the benches were not sufficient for all of you, even if you sat very close together. So when you had to write, there was not enough space, and one half of the class had to go out into the schoolyard and write into the sand. After one hour, it was the other group's turn."

"Oh, yes, now I remember. I always looked for elongated pebbles, because they were better for writing than the round ones," Filora laughed.

"You had red frozen hands and your whole body was jittering," Minawar said. "I can still see it before my eyes, my little daughter cowering in the dust, wrapped up in thick coat and headscarf, and still shivering with cold. It hurt my soul, to see this... and the Chinese kids enjoyed the warmth in their classroom."

"Our teacher, Mrs. Watson, says that a while ago, there had been similar problems with white and black Americans, not much better than with the Han Chinese and Uyghur people in Xinjiang. Why are people like this?"

Minawar took a while to search for an answer, and Filora suddenly began to march in goose step, straight upright, with stiff legs, and swinging her arms up and down.

"Mom, do you remember," she laughed. "We had to march like this in the schoolyard, like soldiers."

She hopped a few steps and grinned,

"I wonder what the teachers would have said if we threw our red scarves into the air as we did today with our mortarboards? Maybe they would have put us in jail."

A thunderstorm of bad memories flashed through Minawar's mind.

"Don't laugh, dear," she said softly. "This is no laughing matter."

Burhanidin

Mirshat does not like going to school.

"I don't understand a word of what the teacher says," he complains. "It's boring. We have to sit quietly all the time and repeat sentences that I don't understand."

"I know, Mirshat," his mother says, trying to comfort him. "Your teacher is Chinese."

Mirshat had resigned himself a long time ago. He no longer tries to follow the lessons and accepts that he, like all other Uyghur children, is one of the bad students, while the Chinese children in his class are the good students. They always listen attentively when the teacher speaks and they never make a sound except when they have to answer a question. When Mirshat is asked a question, he does not know what to answer, because he did not understand what he had been asked. And his tongue is not able to master the complicated pronunciation of the few words he knows, even if he tries. But anyway, he has long since stopped trying. Some of his Uyghur classmates do try and they struggle to learn the difficult Chinese words so that perhaps one day they might be able to switch over to the side with the good students. But Mirshat thinks this is silly and needless, for he would never get the same good marks as the Chinese children, and therefore would never have the chance for a good education and a good job. And that is why he might as well look out the window and daydream. Later, when he grows up, he might help his father in his little herb and tea shop. Or maybe he will become a shepherd, for with sheep you do not need to speak at all.

Mirshat lives with his family in the suburbs of Kashgar, an old, historically important town in the far west of the Xinjiang Uyghur Autonomous Region. His uncle Burhanidin is also

133

from Kashgar, but he was away for many years. He studied linguistics in Beijing and in Turkey, and after that he got a scholarship at an American university where he continued his studies. Then, the university offered him a doctoral scholarship and presented him with the prospect of a bright academic career. But Burhanidin declined.

He declined the scholarship, although his professional knowledge met with great interest all over the world, and nothing fascinated him more than the origins and development of a language and the interrelations of different languages and language families. But during his studies, he had increasingly focused his interest on a question that seemed to be even more important: What is the significance of language for a people? He knew the old languages that had flown into his own mother tongue, the Uyghur language, and the more he knew about these old languages and cultures, the more he came to the conviction that it was of the utmost importance for a people to keep its own language alive.

But the Uyghur language was in danger.

Burhanidin declined the tempting offer of the American university and returned home. Here he wanted to do something to protect his mother tongue. And he had to do it here, not in a foreign country. And not by means of theoretical research but with practical deeds. Yes, he would see to it that Uyghur children did not lose the ability to speak Uyghur. They had every reason to be proud of their people and their culture. He began to make plans for how to achieve his dream.

"Burhanidin," his friends had warned him. "Stay here in America and continue your research. Here you can teach and learn whatever you want. You don't need to be afraid of anybody, here there are no restrictions, no spying by the secret service. Here, science ranks first, not politics."

"For me the living language ranks first."

"Write your dissertation about linguistics. That is also important."

134

"Yes, it is important, but it is more important that there will still be Uyghurs who speak their own language. What is the use of knowing the past, if there is no future?"

Many times he had discussed this with fellow countrymen and colleagues, with professors, philologists and ethnologists. They all advised him to stay. His work was important, they said, and life in America was good and secure. In China, he would not be able to do and say what he thought was important and right. There he would be under constant observation by the secret police.

"I can't just look after my own interests. You know what is going on with education in Xinjiang. The Uyghur language is disappearing from the schools. Even in primary schools and kindergartens the children have to speak Chinese. But the language is our backbone. We need it. If our language dies, our culture will die, too. And then we Uyghurs will become Chinese one day, not on an equal footing and mostly not looking like "real" Chinese, but who even knows..."

Burhanidin had watched with great sadness the Uyghur language being progressively eliminated from school education. Once, parents could choose whether they sent their child to a Chinese or a Uyghur school, but nowadays in many places there were no Uyghur schools anymore, and where there were still Uyghur teachers on the staff, they had to speak Chinese with their students, even outside the classroom.

"It is grotesque!" Burhanidin fulminated, his anger causing the sweat to run down his forehead. This sober-minded thinker could not remain calm when this subject came up. He treasured being Uyghur with all his heart and soul and was proud of his people. He wanted to do everything in his power to save his language and culture, even if it was only a small contribution.

He knew the Chinese Constitution and the Law on Regional National Autonomy very well. Under these laws, ethnic minorities have the right to use and develop their own languages and scripts. So, legally speaking, Uyghurs in Xinjiang have the right to autonomy not only in economic planning, science, culture, arts and religion, but also in the use of their language. The law explicitly provides that in government institutions, "the language of the ethnic group exercising regional autonomy should be used primarily." In Xinjiang, this is the Uyghur language. But Uyghur children are now required to speak only Chinese in school. If parents do not insist on speaking their mother tongue at least at home and upholding the old traditions, their children will very soon lose their own language.

"Nobody can forbid me to protect the Uyghur language! Nobody has the right to prevent me from doing so!" Burhanidin said. And the only person in the whole world, who would have been able to do so, did not do it: Merhaba, his wife. She did not do it because she knew her husband very well, and she knew that his soul would wither if he could not pursue his dream. And so, one evening she had said, "Okay, Burhanidin, let's go home."

On a warm afternoon in late summer, Burhanidin and his former fellow students Barat and Nazirkom were walking through the streets of old Kashgar. He had not been here for many years and it nearly broke his heart to see how it had changed. He knew that the Kashgar city council had decided some years ago to tear down the small mud-walled homes and to replace them with new, modern houses, houses that would better withstand earthquakes than the old houses, which had survived all earthquakes for two hundred years or more. Houses, the government said, that would be built in the traditional style, yet with new sanitary installations and all modern comforts, in which the inhabitants could not help but be happy. Burhanidin, however, did not like them. They were not attractive and the plaster was already flaking off the walls. The three friends passed dilapidated buildings and piles of rubble, and saw children playing in the ruins that had once been their home.

136

"This is the way they treat not only Kashgar's old township but also our language," Burhanidin said, distressed. He had difficulty holding back his tears and he did not know whether these tears were tears of sadness, anger or bitterness. "They are destroying our entire culture!"

"And they do it on purpose," Barat confirmed. "They destroy the narrow, crooked alleyways, so that they can put people in regular, clearly arranged apartment buildings where it's easier to control them."

"There could be a terrorist hiding in the crooked corners," Nazirkom grinned cynically. "Or a separatist..."

"Shut up, Nazirkom! Don't forget that Big Brother might be watching you at every corner."

"What?!" Burhanidin exclaimed. "Are there listening posts in the streets?"

"Sure. What do you think? There are probably far more now than in the old times of Mao and technology has since improved a lot. You never know where these little gadgets might be. You can't see them, but they are there, you can be sure of that."

"Do you see that loudspeaker over there? I bet it is not only a loudspeaker but it can hear as well. A loudspeaker with ears," Nazirkom joked. He never could be serious for long. "But, after all, let them hear what we say. Let them hear what we think of all this idiocy. Come on, let's go to a tea house and celebrate Burhanidin's return."

"And now tell us the truth, old boy. Why did you come back?" Barat asked when they sat down at one of the low tables in the smoky tea house. "Why did you give up your good life in America? You hit the jackpot! A scholarship, freedom, international recognition, security. What are you doing here, where you have to think twice before you utter a word, if you don't want to wake up one morning in prison? Here you have to struggle with Chinese and Uyghur officials whenever you want do something. Here your beloved Uyghur literature and language are beginning to vanish into thin air."

"Exactly. That's why. We must not allow them to disappear!"

"How do you want to prevent it?"

"I will see to it that there are schools where children are taught in Uyghur."

"You're crazy."

"Chinese as the second language, Uyghur as the first language."

"You're crazy."

"First I will start a kindergarten, a kindergarten where children are allowed to speak as their parents, grandparents and all their ancestors have always spoken."

"And you think you can do it just like that?"

"Yes. It is not forbidden to run a private company. That has long been possible."

"And how do you plan to pay for it? Something like that requires a lot of money."

"I will sell my house."

"You're crazy." Not even Barat now had a better answer.

"No. I have given it very serious thought. I have a precise plan, because I think..."

"I think you lost your mind, over there in America."

"No, Nazirkom. But I learned that every single person has to do something if we want to achieve or prevent something. And I am prepared to do everything I can to prevent our children and grandchildren forgetting that they are Uyghurs."

"And you believe you can do it with a kindergarten?"

"It is only a beginning," Burhanidin defended himself. His dark eyes glittered earnestly. "There are many people who are worried about the situation. We are not the only ones. We could create an initiative, an association of like-minded people, find allies, sponsors. We could..."

"We?"

Burhanidin looked at his companions. His eyes went from one to the other, to Barat, then to Nazirkom, and once more to Barat, and then he said in a low voice,

"Why not?"

A deep silence descended on the small table in the tea house and the three men stared into their tea cups, lost in thought. None of them dared to move. None of them dared to look at the others. Each was wrapped in his own thoughts. Burhanidin knew what his friends thought, but he did not want to press them to follow him on this hazardous path. Barat and Nazirkom knew that Burhanidin was right in fearing that the policy of Sinicization would destroy their culture if nobody did anything about it. On the other hand: What could they do? A kindergarten in Kashgar was not enough, and even that would mean overcoming a lot of obstacles: requests, applications, declarations, Chinese functionaries, Uyghur officials, bribes, permits, funding.

"Everything begins with the language."

"And ends in prison," Nazirkom added.

"Nonsense. We won't do anything illegal. We Uyghurs have a right to take part in the decision-making in education and culture. The Uyghur language is guaranteed by law. So, how could it be forbidden to speak Uyghur in a school? Can you tell me?"

"Because there are things that are above the law."

"That's not possible!" Burhanidin retorted. "That can't be! Besides, we don't want... I mean, *I* don't want to provoke the government. I don't want to do anything against the government, I simply want Uyghur children to be allowed to speak their own language. And if there are no public schools which allow it, I will open a private one."

"They won't let you."

"They must let me. It is my right!"

Again, the three friends were silent.

Anyway, there was not much left to say. Burhanidin had explained to his friends what he had decided to do, and this was not easy to digest. Barat and Nazirkom had to collect their thoughts and each would have to decide whether to leave him on his own with his project or not. They knew that it was impossible to hold him back, they had seen it in his eyes. He had abandoned his secure life in America in order to launch a preposterous undertaking in China. Had he forgotten that the rules were different here from those in a democratic country? Did he not remember that reality and the law were not necessarily one and the same? Was his plan pure lunacy or courage? Was it damned to failure or the beginning of a new era?

Some days later, Barat and Nazirkom left for Urumchi, where they worked as teachers. They taught Uyghur literature and without their mother tongue, their profession made no sense. Even now, their position at school was not secure – the curriculum was cut, lessons canceled, teachers thrown out. If the Uyghur language were to disappear completely from the public schools they would not have a job.

Before their departure, none of them broached the delicate subject again, but a seed had been planted in fertile soil.

Burhanidin met teachers, parents, and experts. He talked with them for nights on end. He wrote petitions and applications, made calculations and plans, filled in forms. He collected e-mail contacts, established a website and wrote blogs. He carried out surveys, solicited support and donations, looked for assistants and a suitable location. He filed an official application to open a private Uyghur-language kindergarten and got official permission to do so.

The rent for the premises he had chosen was not too high. A good location, a first step. Of course, there would be some renovations to do. The walls had to be painted. He could do that himself. Merhaba would like to help, and his brother and his children, too. Mirshat, his eldest nephew, was a passionate do-it-yourselfer and he would finally have a job he loved doing. He did not like school, he had confessed to his uncle. It was all rubbish, he said, and anyway he didn't understand a word of what the teachers said. What a pity, Burhanidin thought. The boy is clever and smart. He could have a wonderful future if it were not for this language problem. It crushes his delight in learning. He will not finish school with a qualification, and later there will be no place for him in society. This is exactly what we must avoid. But maybe this is exactly what the government wants to achieve with its educational system?

"A kindergarten only for Uyghur children, you said?" the landlord interrupted his thoughts.

"Of course, we will also accept Chinese children if they want to learn Uyghur. And Kazakh or Kirghiz children..."

"Is it allowed?"

"Sure. I have official permission to open this kindergarten. I showed you the letter the other day, don't you remember?"

"Yes, yes, I have it here. Well, a Uyghur kindergarten... Well, of course, it's a nice idea. There are lots of children... Okay, well, I'll think it over and I'll call you back, okay?"

He did not call back.

Burhanidin did not know what to think. The man was a Uyghur, but he did not want to rent his premises to Uyghur children. Was the pressure of the local government so strong that he might have problems if he did? Burhanidin did not like the idea, though his American friends had warned him. They had said,

"They will find a reason to prevent it. If they cannot find a legal reason, there will be something else. Anything. Any little trifle. You will see. They will never ever allow you to do something that contradicts their interests."

"But we bear responsibility for our people," he had always replied. "What will become of them, if all of the academics go to foreign countries and enjoy life while the ordinary people stay at home and are driven into the furthermost corner of society or are turned into second-class Chinese?"

Burhanidin had not ignored the warning, but he had been so full of his mission that he had thought he would be able to overcome all the bureaucratic and political obstacles by pure enthusiasm and energy.

"And if anything happens to me," he had said to those who meant well, "my brother will take care of Merhaba. She is on my side. She knows that I must go my own way, come what may. She knows that it is dangerous but we will try together. We *must* try."

So Burhanidin went his own way. He found alternative premises. He repaired, cleaned and swept, painted walls and mended holes, bought little tables, chairs, toys and books. He hired an additional kindergarten teacher, and advertised for the newly opened kindergarten. Merhaba now wore a head-scarf. In America, she had not done so, but here most Muslim women did and she wished to openly demonstrate her ethnic origins.

In the first few weeks, everything went well. The children loved to come, and they played and learned with eagerness. The parents were happy that they could talk with their sons and daughters in their own language, while other parents hardly understood what their children were saying, because they mixed the two languages to a gibberish that was hardly comprehensible.

Then, one day, there was an invitation to tea.

Burhanidin was to meet a certain Mr. Imin in a small tea house in the old city. Mr. Imin greeted him amiably and led him to a table where three other men were sitting. Two of them were Chinese, the other one a small Uyghur with a clean-shaven face and short-cut hair.

"Please, sit down, Mr. Ahat," this man said.

Burhanidin took a seat.

"We are pleased that you have found your way back to your homeland."

"Thanks. I'm glad, too."

"We heard that you have successfully finished your studies in America."

"Yes, that's right. I got my master's degree."

"But you did not want to continue your studies? You declined a scholarship."

Burhanidin gave a start. He hardly could hide his amazement. How did they know? Does this mean that he had been observed by the secret service during all those years abroad?

"What was it like in America? What did you do? Tell us about your experiences."

When the invitation had arrived, Burhanidin had already suspected that this meeting was not meant to be a friendly get-together but more of an interrogation. Nevertheless, he pretended to be unsuspecting and began to talk about his linguistic research and the American university system, though he knew quite well that this was not what the four men were interested in.

"Did you meet any fellow-countrymen? Did you have contact with other Uyghurs?"

"Ah," Burhanidin thought, "this is what they want to know." Evasively he answered,

"I always tried to blend in with the local society and to speak the language of the country as much as possible. That's important," he explained, "if you really want to be accepted, especially in the professional field." And before one of the men could ask another question, he added with an engaging smile,

"The only thing I missed in America was our good tea."

"Oh yes, of course, how impolite we are," Mr. Imin apologized and beckoned to the waiter.

After they had chatted a while about tea, coffee and the differences in lifestyle habits, one of the two Chinese asked,

"You recently opened a private kindergarten?"

"Yes, that's right. We already have two groups, each with twelve children aged between two and six years. It's going quite well."

"The two teachers are Uyghur women?"

"Yes, my wife and a young girl from the neighborhood."

"Ah."

The other Chinese said casually, "We have heard that they only speak Uyghur with the children. Is that right?"

"Yes," Burhanidin replied as if it was the most natural thing in the world, but he knew quite well that this was a very dangerous point.

"The children must be prepared for school," the small Uyghur with short hair said. "How will they be able to follow the lessons if they don't know the language?"

Burhanidin hesitated. He would have liked to have answered, "I wish they could speak Uyghur at school, too." But probably it was better to be careful and to search for more subtle explanations. At the end, he did not need to answer at all, because Mr. Imin said,

"It would be better if you engage a teacher who speaks perfect Chinese. Then your kindergarten will continue to flourish." Which meant nothing but, "If you insist on speaking only Uyghur with the children, the kindergarten will be closed!"

It was not the only threat. Burhanidin received anonymous letters and more invitations to tea, and each time he was told in friendly-menacing words that this country did not want to have non-Chinese kindergartens and schools. The law, of course, was inviolable. The law would always take first place, but... He could always count on support, even financial support, he need not worry. Burhanidin, however, understood very well what they did not say in words.

From time to time, unknown persons lurked around the playground, and Merhaba became scared. Her husband instead

144

became increasingly brave, the more they tried to intimidate him. He became a fighter.

Very soon after their visit to Kashgar, Barat and Nazirkom had decided to support Burhanidin and to open a Uyghur-language kindergarten in Urumchi too. They had found many proponents who gave them backing and supported their plans with generous funds. The permission of the Urumchi authorities, however, failed to materialize and the threats in Kashgar became increasingly obvious. The internet activity of the three active men had drawn the township authorities' attention and was monitored carefully.

Burhanidin had now become a well-known personality. All over Xinjiang many people were worried about the future of their language. Many feared that the Uyghur culture and history would soon be forgotten, if their children and grandchildren only learned what the Chinese government wanted them to learn and if their thinking was compressed into the narrow track of the Party's ideology. The rich and millennia-long history, the traditions, art and religion, all this would be buried by the Chinese culture, perhaps extinguished forever. Wasn't it true that the government wanted all people in China to think the same way and blindly follow the way of the Communist Party? Thousands of sympathizers answered to Burhanidin's internet articles. They encouraged him in his resolve and they endorsed the establishment of Uyghur-language schools. The blogs and discussions spread across the entire country, so that the local authorities felt impelled to do something about it.

"Private individuals are not allowed to run schools," a letter said.

"It is illegal to collect donations for private purposes," said another.

The three friends founded a company to facilitate the organization, financing and management, and to give their project the semblance of an economic enterprise. They asked experienced businessmen for help, ensured that the book-keeping was clean and complied with all official regulations. They printed brochures, printed T-shirts with their logo, and sold local products like honey and jam to advertise the school and raise money. But the permits for a kindergarten in Urumchi and a primary school in Kashgar did not materialize. The authorities kept demanding further documents. Time and again they sent them away.

And then, one early morning, there was a knock at the gate.

Burhanidin crossed the yard and opened. Two men were waiting in front of the gate.

"Burhanidin Ahat?"

"Yes."

"Come along with us."

"Where to?" Of course, he knew immediately where to, but he wanted to gain some time.

"I need to tell my wife. Please, wait a moment."

"No, you come now!"

One of the men took his arm and pulled him onto the street. Burhanidin was an intellectual fighter but was helpless against physical violence. He followed the men without saying a word, let them push him into their car and pull him out in front of the police station. Then they brought him into a small room and closed the door. He waited.

Merhaba wondered why her husband did not come for breakfast. She had seen him cross the yard when there had been a knock, but he had not answered when she asked who the early visitor was.

"Burhanidin?"

No answer.

She stepped out into the yard, she asked Burhanidin's brother and his wife, the children. Nobody had seen him. She passed the gate, which was no longer locked, and looked left and right.

"What happened?" she suddenly heard the neighbor asking. "Why did they take Burhanidin away?"

"Take away? Who took him away?" Merhaba's knees went weak, her whole body began to tremble and she felt herself plunging into a deep abyss. She knew with absolute certainty what had happened. Burhanidin had been arrested! She ran back to the house and cried,

"They've put him in prison! Oh, Allah, what shall we do?"

The family members all came into the kitchen and looked at each other aghast. Helpless. What could they do? Nothing. They could only hope that he had been taken in for questioning and would come back home soon. Only hope and wait.

The same morning, the kindergarten was closed. Policemen came and said, "Send the children home." They lined up at the entrance, rigid and transfixed like tin soldiers, impassive, conscious of their power. They waited until the little intimidated band and the two women had left the compound. Then they locked the door and stuck a piece of paper on it.

At the same time, Barat and Nazirkom were arrested in Urumchi. Their company was shut down and the accounts closed.

One morning a man came to Merhaba.

"I know Burhanidin", he said.

Blood surged to Merhaba's face and her hands began to tremble.

"Where is he?" she stammered, nervously. "How is he? Why... Oh, please, come in."

She locked the gate carefully after the man had entered.

"How is Burhanidin? Where did you meet him?"

"We were in the same prison cell for a few days."

"In prison? Which prison? Nobody has ever told us where he is."

"I have just come from Urumchi, I was imprisoned there, for seven years..."

She watched the man curiously. He was thin and pale. He, too, trembled and he hesitated to follow her into the house.

"Come in, please, come and take a seat. I will make some tea."

They sat down at the kitchen table.

"Please, tell me: How is my husband?"

"I did not talk with him much."

"But how is he, what about his health? What did they accuse him of?"

"They want to know who is behind it."

"Behind what?"

"Well, the company... the money."

"I don't understand. Why should there be somebody behind it?"

"I don't know."

They were silent for a while. Merhaba got up, put the kettle on the fire and put a plate of bread and fruit on the table. She watched the man, who sat there in front of her, sad and pale, and who did not dare serve himself. She moved the plate nearer to him. He did not look up and did not say a word. She would have loved to bombard him with questions. She wanted to know so many things, she wished to know everything, but there was something in this man which prevented her from doing so. He seemed to be so vulnerable, as if every question that she posed was like a stab with a knife. But there was one thing that she absolutely had to know. This one question tormented her so much that she could not spare him,

"Has he been tortured?" she whispered anxiously.

"I don't know... they often took him away for interrogation..."

"And then?" When there was no answer, she asked, "What did they do to you?"

The man took a piece of bread and absent-mindedly crumbled it onto the table.

"Now I am free," he murmured without looking at Merhaba.

"Please, tell me more about Burhanidin. Will he be set free too? Will he be brought to trial? What have they accused him of?"

"He didn't talk much."

Merhaba read in the haggard face, the unsteady look and the crooked shoulders that this man was not going to talk much either.

"But he must have said something. Does he at least know what he is charged with?"

"He asked me to visit you as soon as I am free."

"Thank you! I thank you with all my heart, because for three months now we haven't known where he is. Of course, we realized that he had been arrested, but not why and where he is imprisoned. We could not get any information about that. Nobody gave us even the faintest clue. He might just as well have been dead. Who knows what they do to people who try to do something good."

"I have to go now," the man said and got up.

Merhaba escorted him across the yard and opened the gate. She wanted to thank him again and wish him good luck, but he turned away and shuffled away, like a broken, old man.

***

January went by but there was no trial. Then February and March. Summer came again and nothing happened. Time passed sadly and slowly. Merhaba continued to wait in vain for news of her husband and Mirshat continued to go to school without learning anything.

Amangul

It had been an exhausting day. Amangul sat down on the soft felt carpet, leaning comfortably against the pillows of colorful Atlas silk that she loved so much. She also had a dress made of this material, but she wore it only on special days like the Feast of Breaking the Fast or the Feast of the Sacrifice. On normal days when she worked as a farmer's wife from morning till night on her feet and hardly found a minute idle, she did not need beautiful dresses. Now she was tired and she looked forward to a moment of rest. Luckily, her mother-in-law, Maryangul, cared for the children. They had already had their dinner and were in bed. It was finally quiet in the house.

Tursun should have come home long ago. Why was he away for so long?

Although there was much work waiting in the fields, he met in the morning with Memetjan and Kunahun, because they had to talk about the forthcoming visit of the representatives of the Disciplinary Inspection Commission from Urumchi. For days, no, actually for many months, the three men sat together, trying to gather all of the details about the land conditions of their village. That was the reason why Tursun had less time to work in the fields and it was Amangul who had to see to it. It was exhausting. Yes, it was really very difficult to get all these things done. The fields were not large, but work is not done by itself. She had to tend to everything and there was never enough time. Yet she did not complain, because she knew the importance of the problem which her husband and his two friends tried to solve. It was a matter of existence. The future of the village was at stake.

"Amangul!" She suddenly heard her name called from outside the gate. She jumped up and ran across the yard. Somebody was knocking impatiently at the wooden door, "Amangul, open!"

It was Aliya, Memetjan's wife who lived a few houses further up the road.

"They are gone!" she gasped out of breath.

"What do you mean they are gone? Who is gone?"

"Memetjan is gone. And Kunahun and Tursun," the older woman gasped. "Or did *you* see your husband this afternoon?"

"No," Amangul replied hesitantly. "No, I'm waiting for him."

"You will have a long time to wait! They are gone, all three of them are gone, disappeared without a trace." She was beside herself with excitement, worry and fear. She had already run through the whole village, had asked everyone without getting an answer. Nobody had seen the three men since the morning.

Amangul stared at the other woman in disbelief. She did not know what to say and she could not believe what she was hearing. Tursun would come home at any moment. Perhaps the three men had to finish some very important preparation for tomorrow and had gone somewhere else.

Yakupjan, a neighbor, joined the two women. He had heard the voices.

"What do you say, Aliya? Your husband is gone? What happened?"

"I don't know," she sobbed tearfully. "All three of them have disappeared, swallowed up by the earth. In the morning they met in our house, but then there was a call and they left. Nobody has seen them since then."

"A call? Who called?"

"I don't know. I was in the kitchen. I only saw them taking their papers and going away."

Now Yakupjan became restless, too. A terrible suspicion was coming to his mind, because everyone in the village knew that the next day high officials were coming from Urumchi who wanted to talk with the farmers about their farmland. This was very important! They had been hoping for this opportunity for many years in vain. Until now, no one had ever listened to their complaints. They took their land and sold it. They told the villagers that everything was right, that they had to be content with smaller fields, that there are higher priorities and that the Party knows best what is good for the country and what is not. There was no sense in contesting the Party's decisions. After all, a simple farmer should not interfere with the important work of the authorities.

Tursun, Memetjan and Kunahun, however, were not deterred, but instead began to study the laws. They had written letters to the local authorities explaining their situation and filed complaints without success. They had travelled to Urumchi and last year even to Beijing in order to report the problems they had with the Kashgar city government to the Ministry of Land and Resources. Things finally seemed to get going and now the three men who were to represent the farmers were gone! That was strange...

"What shall we do?" Aliya wailed, interrupting Yakupjan's thoughts.

"I hope that nothing has happened to them! They can't just disappear."

"Did you ask Mr. Hu, the Party Secretary?"

"No."

"Maybe he knows something," Yakupjan said. "You'd better go home in case your husbands call. Where is Kunahun's wife?"

"She's at home with her children. She cannot leave them alone."

Amangul closed the gate and went back into the house. Her mother-in-law was sitting in front of an empty plate at the kitchen table and asked, "Where is Tursun?"

"No one knows where he is. Memetjan and Kunahun did not come home either and no one has seen them since morning."

"My son would never stay away without saying a word!"

"Maybe it has something to do with tomorrow. Maybe they need to prepare things. Maybe..."

"No! Something bad must have happened. Tursun would never keep us waiting needlessly!"

She buried her face in her hands and Amangul saw her shoulders quiver. She should comfort the old woman, but how could she comfort her? What could she say, when she herself did not know where her husband was? Maybe he had been in an accident. Was he still alive? Was he in jail? You often heard things like that. After all, the three friends had challenged the local party secretary, the village headman, and the city council of Kashgar. They had dared to publish their complaints on the internet, and this, the authorities do not like. Was it possible that Mr. Hu was involved in this matter? Amangul sat down beside her mother-in-law and served her a cup of tea.

"Drink some tea, Mother," she said softly. "Tursun will call soon. Maybe he's somewhere where there is no telephone. He will certainly call as soon as he can."

There was no call.

Only Yakupjan, knocking at the gate. He had seen the party secretary, but had no information. Mr. Hu dismissed him with an arrogant smile, saying that the three men probably needed some rest to recover from their family responsibilities and the hard fieldwork. This is understandable, isn't it?

Late in the night Amangul and Maryangul lay down near the children on their mats and tried in vain to sleep. Aliya and Kunahun's wife could not sleep that night either. They were much too worried.

Very early in the morning, just before dawn, the telephone rang.

Amangul was jolted awake. As she jumped up, she caught a foot in her blanket, stumbled, and almost fell from the supa. Trembling with agitation, she picked up the phone. Maryangul was already beside her.

"Yes?"

"It's me..."

"Tursun? Where are you, what..."

"We are in Hotan."

"What does it mean, in Hotan?"

"We are in Hotan, Amangul, really, we..."

"What are you doing in Hotan? How..."

"We're on a sightseeing tour."

"Pardon? A sightseeing tour?"

"Amangul, I can't say much... I'm sorry, I have to go."

Stunned, Amangul looked at her mother-in-law and her mother-in-law looked at her daughter-in-law, and the whole room seemed to be filled with incredulous questions and boundless confusion. Slowly and carefully, as if it were a precious treasure, Amangul put back the phone.

"They are on a sightseeing tour," she said as if she wanted to taste these words in her mouth. "They are enjoying a pleasure trip to Hotan, have driven five hundred kilometers in order to visit a distant city, even though today they are having the most important discussions of their lives. What absurd nonsense! Mother, what does this mean?"

"This can only mean one thing. Sure. Yes, of course, I know it for sure! They have been kidnapped! Mr. Hu is behind it. And probably the guys from Kashgar. Those who have taken away and sold our land. The officials who are only out for money and put it in their own pockets. Yes! It must be. They have kidnapped them! Tursun would never have gone away without letting us know."

"Especially not now!"

Everything was at stake. Today, high officials would come from Urumchi and finally the peasants of Isimsiz could see a little glimmer of hope for justice. For years, Tursun, Memetjan and Kunahun had tried hard to achieve this. They had familiarized themselves with computers to be able to visit countless websites, had read the Property Law of the People's Republic of China, and studied farmers' cooperatives. They had calculated

154

with numbers and written letters. Everything had been in vain. All these years, no one had taken notice of these numbers and letters, because they touched something that was common practice but not legal. Their issue was the sale of land, namely the land that was cultivated by the farmers of Isimsiz, which they desperately needed.

Tursun always kept his wife informed about his enquiries and investigations and thus Amangul knew quite well the facts and which laws they could invoke. All land in China is owned by the State. So it had been from the time of Mao, and so it was today. After the early 1980s, when the people's communes were resolved, all arable land was transferred to village communities as a collective property. Consequently, since then, these collectives owned all the land, and they made contracts with the peasant families allowing these families to cultivate a certain number of fields on their own. The land which had been given to a peasant family could not be taken back just like that. The Agriculture Law of the People's Republic of China, Chapter IX, Article 78, says: "Where the rights and interests of farmers are infringed upon in violation of the provisions of laws, the farmers or agricultural production and operation organizations may, according to law, apply for administrative reconsideration or bring a lawsuit in the People's Court."[1] Thus, the Kashgar officials had no right to sell land on their own authority to Chinese and foreign investors. And now there were new rumors about further sales. The farmers would starve if more land was taken away from them.

"We are peasants," Tursun said again and again. "We have nothing but our land and our labor. We are peasants and not artisans or merchants. We don't even have the money to invest in a new livelihood. With the few yuan we are offered as compensation for our land, we could not even buy a tiny apartment on the outskirts of the city, because the cost would be many

[1]   http://www.npc.gov.cn/englishnpc/Law/2007-12/12/content_1383785.htm

thousands times more. We have nothing but a small piece of land, even now barely sufficient to give food to our children."

Already in the 1980s, thousands of hectares of land given to the village community of Isimsiz had been taken away for the Kashgar airport. Later, the municipality had confiscated thousands more Mu and two years later, again did so in another area, on which soon afterwards modern apartment blocks had been built. After protesting, the farmers received a small amount of compensation, but not enough to build up a new life. They were afraid of further land sales.

When Tursun's letters and complaints remained unheeded, he had written a detailed report on the Isimsiz situation and posted it on the internet. He had quoted the respective legal provisions and supported his concerns and the resultant complaints by facts and figures. The law provides that "People's Courts and the competent administrative organs of justice shall provide legal assistance to farmers in accordance with relevant regulations." But the farmers of Isimsiz had not been asked whether they agreed to sell their land. It had simply been taken away from them and now people from other parts of China – Han Chinese – lived there in modern apartment houses.

Apparently, this report made an impact, for officials from the Discipline Inspection Commission of Urumchi planned to come and check the situation. They did not just want to talk with the responsible officials from Kashgar, the Isimsiz party secretary and the village headman, but also with the three representatives of the farmers who had published the report on the internet. The meeting was scheduled for this afternoon. But now the three men, the only ones who were able to clearly explain their position, were not there. They were in Hotan. They were amusing themselves on a sightseeing trip!

"'What cheek! What irresponsibility!' the officials will say," Amangul moaned. "And Mr. Hu and the officials from Kashgar will confirm, 'Yes, yes, that's always the problem with those

Uyghur farmers. They can complain and protest, but when it comes to work, they are suddenly up and away. On a pleasure trip! Imagine! You surely won't place confidence in such people, gentlemen, will you?' That's how it will be, Mother! Exactly this was their plan!"

Amangul had overcome her first shock and was now ready to fight. If Tursun was not there, *she* would go to the meeting! Her thoughts began to swirl. What was she to do? She had to care for the sheep and goats in the stable and feed the chickens. Her mother-in-law would look after the children and cook the meals. Today, the pomegranates should to be picked, because some were already ripe and had to be sold tomorrow on the bazaar, at least a few baskets. The cow had to be milked and weeds had to be hoed, if they wanted to have good vegetables this year. The fields were small, but they needed constant care. The cotton field could wait. She would see to it in the next few days or maybe when Tursun was back. And once she had cleaned the barn, had checked the fertilizer... oh, actually the donkey cart was supposed to be repaired... Tursun already planned to do it yesterday. Yesterday, when he was traveling to Hotan!

The children were awake. The small Yasim cried because he felt that something was wrong. Aygul, the seven-year-old girl, could help feed the chickens and search for good eggs before she went to school. She was a sensible girl and already a good help in the household. But did she do her homework? Last night Amangul had forgotten to ask, because everything had been such a panic. But, definitely, Aygul was a good student and always did her homework conscientiously.

Would it be difficult to find the necessary files on Tursun's computer? He told her everything about his research and she knew just about everything as well as he and his two companions did, but she would have to find the exact figures and data on the computer. These she did not know by heart. How many inhabitants were there in the village? How many hectares of collective land were left? How many fields did each family have? How much land had already been sold and when? She had to find all these figures. That was important. And, of course, the paragraphs of the respective law. What else?

"I must see Aliya and tell her that Memetjan is in Hotan."

Amangul could not help a nervous giggle. It was absurd. The regional government sent high officials to her small village wishing to talk to men who were not there, because they had decided to make a trip precisely on this day, and she, a young Uyghur peasant woman who should actually take care of the home and children, was preparing for this meeting. She, Amangul, Tursun's wife, planned to take the whole thing into her own hands. Would Aliya come with her? If they were two, it would be easier, but actually Aliya was not the right person for such a thing. She was a simple woman who could work hard, but did not understand complicated official matters. Neither could Sarigul, Kunahun's wife. Oh, yes, she too had to be informed. Unfortunately she lived quite far away and had no phone. Perhaps Aliya could run to her.

Thus her thoughts leaped hither and thither, as she knocked at Memetjan's yard gate. It took a long time before she heard steps coming closer. Maybe Aliya had still been asleep. It was hardly dawn.

"Do you already know? Did Memetjan call you?"

The woman stared at her blankly. She looked tired and depressed. Perhaps she had not slept at all tonight.

"Call? No..."

"Do you know where they are? In Hotan!" A beaming smile flew over Amangul's face. She took the older woman in her young, strong arms and laughed merrily, "Imagine, Aliya, imagine! They travelled to Hotan yesterday, for a sightseeing tour. Just for fun!"

"No."

"No, of course not. But they are actually in Hotan. That's true."

Aliya did not know what to think. What was Amangul talking about? Had the poor young thing lost her mind, out of sheer desperation and concern about her Tursun? Memetjan had never travelled. He was not interested in foreign areas, and big cities frightened him. He did not even like to go to the Sunday livestock market in Kashgar, when he needed a sheep or a cow. And when from time to time he did, he complained afterwards about the terrible noise, the many cars, the impatient people.

"No, this can't be," she said, and freed herself softly from her neighbor's hug.

"Yes, yes, Aliya, believe me. Tursun just called." Her words bubbled out of her. "He could not say much, he immediately hung up again. I guess somebody was watching him."

"Why?"

"Why? Well, because he was *not allowed* to tell me the truth! Because he was under guard. Don't you understand, Aliya? Our husbands have been kidnapped. They have been kidnapped, so that they cannot speak with the officials from Urumchi today. Do you understand me? Somebody has kidnapped them and locked them up somewhere in Hotan in a hotel. Or maybe in a prison."

"In a prison...?"

"No, I don't think so, probably in a hotel room. Otherwise Tursun would not have been able to use a telephone. But they are under observation, that's clear. They are not there voluntarily."

Slowly Aliya began to realize that her impetuous, young neighbor might actually be right.

"You mean... Amangul, that cannot be true... you mean, someone has brought Tursun, Memetjan and Kunahun to Hotan, so that they cannot explain how much of our land has been taken away?"

"Precisely. Why else? Why the only three men who can prove all this? And why now when they finally have the chance to be heard. Mr. Hu and the officials from Kashgar are afraid of them! Yes, they are afraid. They know very well that it was all illegal. They're afraid that their illegal manipulations will be revealed and they will have to explain where the money has gone."

"And now?"

"And now I will do it. Aliya, I know everything. Tursun always told me what he found out, and all the proof is somewhere on his computer. I only need to find them."

Amangul was jiggling on her feet. Full of impatience and energy, she could not stand still and her thoughts jumped far ahead. Hungry sheep and pomegranates that had to be picked – now there was no place for them in her head. Now there were more important things to do.

"Could you please go to Sarigul and tell her that our husbands are fine?" Amangul asked with an impish smile. "Tell her that they are on a pleasure trip in Hotan." But when she saw Aliya's confused look, she quickly added, "No, dear, tell her only that they are doing well and that they will come home soon."

The day had not yet began to dawn. On a nearby farm a cock crowed and another one answered from somewhere. The muezzin called for prayer. She had plenty of time until noon, but there were also many things to do. The sheep and goats could not wait and the cow had to be milked, but everything else would have to wait. Luckily her mother-in-law would take care of the house as she usually did. Tursun's father had died last year, far too young. Amangul missed him very much, not only because he had been a kind man who could tell wonderful stories, but also because the work in the fields was too much for one man alone. She often had to help her husband.

The corn soup for breakfast was already cooking on the stove when Amangul entered with the milk bucket.

"So, now we have to bury all hope of justice," Maryangul said in a dark mood. "This was our last chance."

"No, Mother," Amangul replied. "I will go to the meeting."

"You? What do you want to do there?"

"I'll explain to the inspectors that our land was sold illegally and that we have received far too little compensation, and that all further violation of our contracts must be prevented."

With an unusual self-confidence and with an irresistible glow in her dark eyes, she looked at her mother-in-law.

"If our men are not here, we women have to do it!" She put down the milk bucket and seized Maryangul's hands. "Aliya and Sarigul cannot do it, but will *you* come with me?"

"What do you mean? Come where?"

"Yes, Mother. You are strong. Come with me. I will speak with them and you're just there, giving me your strength."

"What do you want to say, dear? How... oh, no, they will never listen to us women. That makes no sense. We don't know anything about these things."

"You bet I do know them! Tursun told me everything. I just need to search for the documents."

Maryangul took the children to school and kindergarten and then she sat down next to her daughter-in-law and tried to help with the preparations.

It was midday. Amangul and Maryangul stood in front of the party secretary's office. They had changed clothes. Amangul now wore her beautiful silk dress and a colorful embroidered doppa and her mother-in-law a simple dark dress with a gold-woven headscarf. They looked appealing, the young and the old woman, and they glowed with pride and confidence. They were going to represent their village and they were determined to do their best. For a moment they hesitated when they noticed the two large black limousines, an extremely rare sight in the village.

"These are the gentlemen from Urumchi," Maryangul whispered.

"Let's go."

They took each other by the hand and entered the building. A police officer was standing next to the door and a young

Chinese, probably the party secretary's new assistant, looked up from his desk and snubbed rudely,

"No office hours now! There is an important meeting starting any moment."

"That's what we are coming for." Amangul's heart almost stood still. She was terribly excited but forced herself to keep talking calmly and firmly, "We have something important to contribute."

"I beg your pardon?"

"We have an invitation for this meeting. Look here."

She handed the man the letter that Tursun had received from the Commission for Discipline Inspection of the Uyghur Autonomous Region.

"You are Tursun Turap?" The man grinned cheekily. "I am very surprised."

"I am his wife."

"And why has Mr. Tursun not come himself when he has such a pretty invitation?"

"He is not here at the moment. I have come in his place."

"If he is not able to come himself, the good Mr. Tursun caught a bad break. He should have better organized his time."

"He has been kidnapped!"

"What are you saying?"

"He has been kidnapped, the same as Memetjan and Kunahun! They were to give a statement before the inspectors from Urumchi concerning the land sales, you know. The inspectors have come to Isimsiz especially to talk with them. It is very important!"

"Well, if it is important, the gentlemen should not have let somebody kidnap them, don't you think?"

"This is no laughing matter! It is true. They have really been kidnapped. I don't know by whom, but perhaps Mr. Hu knows."

Now the man did not grin his snotty grin any longer, but jumped up from his chair, banged his fist on the table and

shouted at the women, "Get out! How dare you! You're not seriously claiming that Mr. Hu might have something to do with
a kidnapping! Get out of here at once!"

"No!"

The door of the meeting room opened a crack and the party
secretary peered out.

"What's going on?"

"Nothing."

"Oh, yes, there is something!" Amangul squeezed past the assistant and said, "Mr. Hu, it is important. I need to talk to the
men from Urumchi. Please, let me in. I am Tursun's wife. He
and his two comrades are not here today, but I can represent
them. I have all the documents here."

"Where are the three men?"

"They have been kidnapped."

The two Chinese looked at each other, but their eyes were
bland. Neither of them had the slightest emotion in them. No
surprise, no anger, no satisfaction, and no mockery. And yet
Amangul had the vague feeling that she could grab their mockery with her hands. They knew it! Yes, they had known that
her three opponents would not appear today to testify against
them. Against them and the responsible officials from Kashgar. The party secretary closed the door behind him with the
utmost caution, so that no one in the other room could hear
what was said.

"Kidnapped?" asked Mr. Hu with an indulgent smile. "What
gives you this unusual idea? Who would kidnap three little farmers from Isimsiz?"

Amangul was on the point of punching him in the face.

"You, of course! You and your accomplices from Kashgar!"
But she had to control herself if she wanted to achieve anything at all.

"The hijackers cannot expect much ransom money," the party
secretary smirked, and the assistant smiled at his superior's wit.

"Oh, no, that's nonsense, madam. Go home and do not worry. Your husband will surely come home soon."

Of course he will come home, thought Amangul, but only when it's too late to convince the inspectors of your illegal land sales.

"I have documents that I must submit to the gentlemen from Urumchi."

"You must do nothing whatsoever! Go now! Go, please, young lady. Go and take care of your home. I have things to do!" And when Amangul still did not give up, holding her papers in her hand, he added a little louder, "Did you not understand me? I have things to do!"

The door of the meeting room opened again and a stranger looked out and asked, "Can we start now?"

This was the opportunity! She could push Mr. Hu aside, slide the documents into the man's hand and say here was the proof, that in these papers he could read in full detail how many times the village had been cheated, how much land had been sold illegally. But she hesitated a moment too long.

"Yes, of course, sir," the party secretary nodded to the stranger zealously. As Maryangul saw a dangerous flash in Amangul's eyes, she put an appeasing hand on her arm, because she feared a disaster. Mr. Hu already had slipped through the door, and before he closed it behind him, he turned once again to his assistant and said, "See to it that the ladies leave the office. I don't want any further disturbances."

Amangul and Maryangul were standing undecided, hand in hand next to the desk. The chance was gone! The only second in which they might have had the opportunity to tell the truth was missed. Over and out, too late! The assistant pushed them impatiently to the door. They did not resist. They let it happen in silence, in silence and shame. They had not been able to prevail against the slippery, cunning, slick self-confidence of Mr. Hu.

"And not a word about this absurd talk of kidnapping! Do you understand? Such rumors may be dangerous. Very dangerous... very dangerous..."

Slowly, the two women walked back home through the quiet village road. Those they met wondered about their fine clothes and would have liked to ask the reason for wearing them, but Amangul and Maryangul just gave a short greeting and continued silently their way. Their neighbor Yakupjan saw them coming and shouted from afar, "The officials from Urumchi are here but our village representatives are not! Did you find out where they are? Do you know what happened?"

They nodded to him, but did not answer.

Two days later, when it was already evening, Tursun came home. A large black car dropped him off in front of the gate. He closed it behind him. Amangul saw him coming across the courtyard with clumsy steps. He was carrying a bag that she had never seen before, and somehow the whole of him had changed. He looked tired and empty. Hesitantly, she went to meet him, but then she stopped and waited. Was that her courageous husband, the resolute and fearless man who was untiringly fighting for what he thought was right? This man who was shuffling so slowly and sadly across the yard? They looked at each other without saying a word. Then Amangul asked with a look at the new bag,

"You have been shopping there, in Hotan?"

"Things for sleeping," he replied listlessly. "They gave it to us." And after he stared for a while at his bag, he said, "It was all in vain!"

"Yes, it was all in vain. But at least you are back home and not in prison."

"It was like prison."

"Daddy, daddy is back!" the children cried, and came running towards him. They rushed into his arms and chattered merrily, while he patted them and tried to smile. "Come on, children, we must not let your grandmother wait any longer."

Later in the evening, when the children were asleep and the adults sat together on the supa, Tursun began to tell his story. They had received a call three days ago during their final preparations. Someone promised to give them a document that could prove the legitimacy of their claims. When they arrived shortly afterwards at the agreed place, two men were waiting in a big black car and urged them to get in. The doors locked automatically, and then they drove for hours on the highway that leads from Kashgar, along the southern edge of the desert, to Hotan. They passed all checkpoints unhindered. Apparently, the sentries had been informed beforehand. And when the three friends asked their captors what was happening, they got no other answer but "Our task is to bring you to Hotan. You have three days to visit the city. Then we will bring you back – if you don't do something stupid."

"We didn't see any of the city," Tursun went on. "We sat in a small hotel room and could only look out the window or at the television set, which received only one single station and was constantly flickering. Once our guards drove us around to the large People's Square so that we could admire the huge statue of Mao and Uncle Kurban. 'That's as it should be,' they warned us. 'Even though the Great Chairman is no longer alive, every citizen in China ought to feel great gratitude towards the Party.' That was it. That was our pleasure trip to Hotan."

"And do you know what Amangul has done?" Maryangul asked. "You can be proud of her."

Tursun looked at his pretty wife with tenderness.

"Yes, I know. Alone with all that hard work, especially now at the end of summer, when so many things have to be done. And I was not there, I simply went away. I'm sorry, Amangul. I know how hard it must have been for you."

"Not only that. She did something else and she almost succeeded."

"It was nothing," Amangul protested, embarrassed. "After all we didn't succeed."

"But you tried!" Tursun's mother reported in great detail about the most exciting day she had experienced since her youth during the Cultural Revolution. "And in the end he kicked us out," she concluded. "He literally kicked us out!"

"I should have pushed him away! He is a disgusting, vile wretch who thinks he can get away with anything." Anger flashed in Amangul's eyes at the memory of this shameful moment when she had given up too quickly.

"You did what you could, dear. It was very brave, and you showed him that Uyghur women have something in their head. That was great!"

Embarrassed, she lowered her eyes.

"He will see a threat in us, because we know more than we should know."

"His term is soon expired. Then he will get a good post somewhere in the east and make a nice life with lots of money. With our money."

"There will be a new one."

"Yes, there will be a new one, and that one will also stuff his pockets. But I don't think that someone will dare again to touch our land. The Discipline Inspection Commission will keep an eye on our village."

They sat in silence for a while, then Amangul wondered, "Everybody in the village will ask why you were away for three days. They must think that you shrank back from the confrontation, that you were scared and let them down, like cowards."

"Shall I say that we just felt like visiting the big Mao statue in Hotan? On the very day that we finally had the opportunity to assert our right before a higher authority? Because we wanted to go on a sightseeing tour? Then we wouldn't be able to look in their eyes ever again."

"And if you told the truth?" Amangul asked.

"Then we'll find ourselves in prison sooner or later. That's for sure. They threatened us, just like you. And they will always find a reason. After all, we are dealing not only with Mr. Hu, but also with the officials from Kashgar."

"Then you say nothing and life will go on as it always has," suggested Maryangul. "People will forget about it. In any case, no one really expected that things would change. The strong ones are always right, it is not so? We've been through so many things and life has always gone on."

"This time we had a real chance," Tursun protested. "The central government wants to take more strict action against corruption and it would not have been the first time that an official is called to account and punished. That's why the Discipline Inspection Commissions have been established. However..." He paused for a moment, then continued, "However, if they are hindered in their investigations... well, Mother, I'm going to talk tomorrow with Memetjan and Kunahun. Maybe it's better to be a poor farmer with a wonderful wife than an unsuccessful hero behind bars."

Life went on as Maryangul had predicted. The inspectors from Urumchi had left the same evening. In the documents presented by the local officials there was nothing to complain about. There was no evidence of manipulation or illegal land sales. Everything seemed to have been handled correctly.

Halmurat

In university, Halmurat had always been one of the best students. He wanted to be an internist, preferably specializing in cardiology, because the heart is the center of life. It beats to keep a person alive and when it stops, life ends. But besides its physiological function, it is said in all cultures of the world that the heart is also the place where love resides. Of course, you cannot locate feelings, but the heart can be examined and healed when it is sick. And although this idea was a totally unscientific one, Halmurat loved it and hoped with all his heart that one day he would have the opportunity to work as a cardiologist.

"A human being is much more than just a body," he said to himself. At the university, he had learned the basics of medical knowledge. Later he would be able to apply them to patients and their illnesses, and someday he might also understand the deeper nature of humanity. He wanted to help and cure diseases, but above all he wanted to keep learning, to keep learning about the world and conducting research to open up new possibilities. Heart surgeons could transplant a heart. But what happens to a man when a stranger's heart beats inside him? There were still so many things to explore. He knew very little about the relationship between body and soul. He longed to know more. It was a fascinating subject and he wished to study both aspects of the heart. Was it the ludicrous idea of a young student? Maybe. But Halmurat was a dreamer. He loved this idea and dedicated himself to researching the heart.

In the cardiology department of Korla's big hospital he would surely have the opportunity to gain experience. He applied and was accepted.

"We need you in the first aid station," he was told. Later, when he had gained some practical experience, perhaps he could join another department. At the moment, however, there was no vacancy in the Department of Internal Medicine.

Halmurat was quite content and plunged into the work with enthusiasm. At the first aid station there was a lot to do. Emergency patients arrived constantly, some in ambulances with flashing lights, some in a rented tricycle taxi or on donkey carts, some on foot, supported and comforted by relatives, and some alone. Every day, from morning to evening, and also at night, there was intense activity. The seven doctors, five Han Chinese and two Uyghurs, worked in three shifts of eight hours. If one of them was absent or in case of unusual circumstances, extra shifts were arranged, but often the five Chinese doctors were unable to serve for one reason or another, and the two Uyghur doctors took over the extra shifts.

Halmurat often worked sixteen hours a day. Occasionally, he got a friendly smile from the management, but never extra remuneration or compensatory time off. He accepted it because he hoped for better career opportunities and the possibility of moving to the cardiology department. In addition, the work was important. Many people needed immediate help. He saw every day how to apply his theoretical knowledge in practice and how much pain he could relieve. Only one thing bothered him: "Your identity card, please!"

In the emergency ward no patient was treated before his identity card had been examined, all personal data checked, and the treatment costs paid.

"That is five hundred yuan – for the time being."

Most people who were not working for state authorities or big enterprises could not afford health insurance, and even if they had insurance, they had to advance the costs for medical care and medications and hope that they would get parts of it refunded. And those who have neither insurance nor money must pray to Allah for help.

Halmurat hated this regulation. Sometimes every minute counts when a patient is seriously injured. Or when a traumatized child is crying. But no, no exception! First all formalities, then the treatment. And without payment no treatment at all! Even if you collapse in the street... no exception!

No exception?

Oh, yes, there were exceptions! How often had Halmurat had seen his colleagues taking Chinese patients aside and saying, "All right, all right. We'll do that later..."? But not only that. The treatment was not the same. Uyghurs often had to wait longer, were examined carelessly, had to buy extra medications and underwent additional investigations. And when a man came with a bleeding wound, the police were called, because he might be a troublemaker, or a terrorist.

Once Halmurat had watched a Chinese colleague prescribing the wrong and most expensive drug to a Uyghur woman. When he confronted him later, the doctor only smiled awkwardly and said, "Oh, no, no. You're wrong.... It's all good, everything is okay."

Halmurat knew quite well that he should not criticize a Chinese colleague, for otherwise they would find a reason to urge his dismissal, and then he would never again find a job as a doctor in any other hospital. You cannot criticize a Han Chinese. They are almost like a god, untouchable. At least that is how it seemed to Halmurat and to his Uyghur colleagues.

Therefore, by and by, Halmurat had given up hope of becoming a cardiologist. He still had a keen interest in human hearts, but now rather in a different way. Some were made of stone, those were definitely incurable. Others were deeply hurt and often could be healed by some friendly attention, without any sedative. By now, he had worked for five years in the first aid station and he did not hope any longer for a scientific career. Only Han Chinese could be well-paid specialists and successful researchers, whether they had the same qualifications as their Uyghur colleagues or not.

But as he knew the how the first aid station worked, he volunteered as often as possible for extra shifts. "When I'm here," he said to himself, "I know that all patients are treated equally." Work was not very demanding, and it had soon become routine. He had to sew and bandage wounds, X-ray bones, measure blood pressure and issue medications. It was not at all the kind of work he had once dreamed of. He was passed over by Chinese colleagues. He felt personally discriminated against and exploited. But he was able to help people, and above all he could help all those who came to him, regardless of who they were. That was why he left the hospital every day after work with an uneasy feeling. "What are they doing when I'm not there?"

Yakup was an old man. Actually, he was not more than sixty years old, but he looked and felt like a very old man whose life was behind him. Since his wife had passed away, there was not much that seemed worth living for, but as he still was alive, he had to do something to earn a living. Only Allah gives life and takes it back. Allah had taken his wife's life by telling her heart to stop beating. Perhaps her heart had become sick from hard work or out of concern for the children who had moved to a distant city, or because of the dirty air in this big city, or perhaps long ago during the horrors of the Cultural Revolution. But maybe it had simply been time for her to die. No one but Allah could know.

Now Yakup lived alone, and that for many years. Every morning he went with his three-wheeled handcart to the market, loaded it with fresh fruit and then went to the center of Korla in order to sell it. He worked from early morning until evening, so he earned enough money for a modest living. In the evening he sometimes sat with his neighbors in front of the house or in a warm room, and then, with a small bowl of tea in their hands, they talked about the past day, about life and the world.

172

One ordinary morning, Yakup was pushing his cart to the place where he joined up with several other street vendors. Some of them were Uyghurs, others Chinese, because here in Korla there were more Han Chinese than in most other cities of Xinjiang. Here they make up the majority of the population. They worked for the big companies that have their factories near the city or produce oil and other mineral resources in the Taklamakan Desert, and these companies do not employ Uyghur people. They get their workers from central China. That was the reason why his two sons had left the city. They had not been able to find a job. Again and again they had been told the companies don't hire Uyghurs. Wrinkles of anger appeared on Yakup's forehead and he pushed his cart with a violent jerk over a crumbling hole in the road so that the old wheels began to groan dangerously. But the thought still outraged him: Adil and Ahat had learned a decent profession, they were industrious and diligent, but nobody wanted to give them work. After they had left Korla, Aygul's suffering had worsened, because her heart was now suffering in two ways. But that was already a very long time ago and now Yakup lived his life alone.

He parked the cart, placed a small wooden wedge under the front wheel so that it could not roll off, and piled his yellow figs on large green leaves to make delicious, juicy mountains of fruit, as golden as the sun in the sky. Now, the end of summer, was the best time for yellow figs. They were rare on the market and here he was the only one who sold them. They were a treasure. They tasted as sweet as honey and melted away on the tongue like..., well, like... oh, how long ago that was now... Aygul, so long ago...

"Good morning, Yakup!"

Yakup looked up.

"Good morning, Turap. Have your chickens laid enough eggs?"

"Yes, they were quite busy. Just look." Turap crouched on the ground next to a pile of cardboard boxes filled with white eggs.

"You have a lot of chickens."

"Well, those of my neighbors were also busy."

"Hello, friends," called another man from across the street to them. "Are you hungry? I have wonderful fresh naan bread. My wife just baked it this morning. Should I come over? Wait, just a moment."

Yakup put one of his figs on a green leaf and waited for the bread seller. "A wonderful idea, my friend, thank you."

The bread seller's cart was different from Yakup's cart. It had two large wheels and a colorful umbrella that was attached to the loading board and cast a shadow onto the piles of bread so they wouldn't dry out. He put down a rod to prevent his cart from tipping over and broke one of the large, round loaves into three parts. "A beautiful day today, isn't it?"

"Yes, a beautiful day. Here, try one of my figs. They are the best I've had for a long time."

The man took the yellow-green gift with both hands and a slight nod. Yakup put a second fruit on another leaf and handed it with both hands and a polite nod to his friend Turap.

"Unfortunately, I have no boiled eggs today," Turap said, "and I suppose you wouldn't know what to do with a raw one."

The three men laughed and for a while they ate in silence.

"I miss the donkey carts," Yakup said thoughtfully.

"Some people have now carts with motorbikes."

"Then you need not walk or pedal."

"They are noisy and stinky."

"And how they stink!"

"Naan bread with gasoline smell... or figs.... Well, I've got to go now, my friends. Take care."

"Take care. And have a nice day."

The bread seller folded up the rod and slowly rolled away with his cart. The two other men sat side by side on the ground and watched him.

174

"Look, Turap, the stripes on his umbrella are almost glowing as golden as my figs."

"A nice guy. Did you know him?"

"No. But his bread is really good."

The hours passed. From time to time a customer came and bought a full carton of eggs or only a few, which Turap put carefully into a bag. Others stopped to look at the figs, asking critical questions about freshness and durability. Whenever he could sell some Yakup was pleased, because the soft fruits did not last long. When they are fully ripe, their taste is best, just like today, but you cannot keep them for a long time and you have to be even more careful with them than with Turap's raw eggs.

It was shortly after noon. At some distance a car had stopped and several men got out. Two of them went from one stall to the other, talked with the sellers, and gradually came closer. Now they stood with a Chinese man who sold all kinds of colorful plastic things. Yakup and Turap watched the men suspiciously, because they did not look like customers. Their behavior was more like policemen, but they did not wear uniforms, and at the moment they were chatting quite cheerfully with the Chinese neighbor. They examined his goods and laughed at this and that funny kitsch.

"Your papers!"

Turap winced. The words sounded like a whip striking a stubborn ass into obedience. He stood up and fumbled in his pocket for his identity card.

"The license?"

Turap's hands trembled as he was digging further into his pocket, then he handed a worn piece of paper to the stranger.

"And yours?"

That morning Yakup had not put on his long gray coat, because it promised to be a warm day, and he had forgotten to take out his identity documents and put it into the other pocket. When he had seen the car and the men getting out, he remembered it with horror. Uyghurs must always have their identity card with them, and recently there were more and more controls – without any reason. Chinese were never bothered, only Uyghurs. Yakup did not know the reason, but it embittered him. It was not just. "The Uyghurs are here at home. It was our ancestral land for ages," he said to himself, but he did not complain, and obeyed just like all the others did.

"Your ID! Hurry up!" an impatient voice above him thundered.

Yakup got up with difficulty, holding on his cart. His knees wavered. He wondered how this young rascal could speak in such a tone with an old man, but he answered apologetically, "I do not have it with me today. I have..."

"And your license?"

"That's also..."

"Get away! You have no right to stand here!"

"I am always here."

"Didn't you hear what I said? Get away from here and don't come back! Without documents you have no right to stand anywhere. Did you understand that?"

"I have..."

"Shut up!" the other man intervened impatiently.

Turap tried to explain that his neighbor, the fruit seller Yakup, stood there every day, next to him, and he knew for sure that he possessed a permit for this particular place. For twenty years they had been here selling fruit and eggs.

"Shut up!"

"If you want, you can also pack up your stuff and take off!" the younger man added. "You know quite well that everybody at any time has to be able to prove his identity."

"I did not see that the Chinese next to us has been showing his papers," Turap thought to himself, but he did not say it,

176

because by now a small group of people had gathered around them and an open dispute might have serious consequences. He could lose his license, and then what would he live on?

"Come on, old man, cut out from here, if you don't want us to arrest you!"

Yakup still stood indecisive, torn between rage and helplessness, anger, worry and sadness, defiance and despair.

"I will run home quickly and fetch my papers."

"I told you to get away from here, immediately, and with everything you have!" The man kicked against Yakup's carts so that the fig piles tottered dangerously. One of the fruits rolled down and fell to the ground. The young man crushed it with his foot. A yellow treasure, trampled like dirt. Trampled down like my people... trampled and humiliated. Not by accident or carelessness, but deliberately, in a vile, arrogant awareness of power. And this power was based on nothing but belonging to another race. The bitterness of many years broke its way, defeating Yakup's submissive attitude, "No, this is my place. I have stood here every single day for twenty years!"

With both hands, the younger man grabbed Yakup's cart and knocked it over. Figs, leaves and bills scattered on the ground. Some spectators jumped aside, and a child bent down for a yuan-note, which came flying at his feet. All stared in fear and curiosity at what was coming. The old Yakup was about to pounce blindly on his opponent, the other man pulled him back, they scuffled, and Yakup cried, "My figs... You must not..."

He got a resounding slap in the face.

Yakup stumbled back a few steps and then the man suddenly had a stick in his hand. He slammed. Again... again. Yakup fell down. The spectators held their breath. Women, with shock, put a hand over their mouths. Men stared in silence. Turap bent down to his friend. Yakup did not move. Children collected stray bills and a few figs that were still edible. The two security men set up the cart and dragged it away to their car at the end of the street.

"No!" Yakup pleaded with his last strength. "No, you can't take my cart! It's my cart, my property..." Then he could not say anything more, because blood ran from his forehead into his mouth and he had to spit.

"You must see a doctor, Yakup," Turap whispered and embraced his friend reassuringly. "That's a nasty wound. You're bleeding terribly." He searched for a handkerchief and put it on Yakup's forehead. In an instant it was saturated with blood. He could not stop the bleeding. "Is anyone here who can help? Otherwise he will bleed to death."

A man came closer. The other spectators went their way and did not look back. The figs were trampled down, a yellow mass smeared over green leaves and gray asphalt.

"I'll drive him to the hospital," the man said.

He went away to get his car. Turap picked up the black and white doppa that had fallen from Yakup's head, picked up some last intact figs, wrapped them in the few green leaves that he could find, and saved them near his eggs.

Halmurat had almost finished his shift and today there was no second shift waiting for him. Finally, he would spend a free evening, enjoying it with some friends over lamb kebab and tea.

A new emergency case.

A man with an open head wound was brought in. He seemed to have already lost a lot of blood and was still bleeding heavily. Though somebody had tied a scarf around his head, the bleeding had not stopped.

Colleague Chen took over the new patient. The man who had brought him wanted to leave immediately. He did not know the wounded man, he said, he had just driven him to the hospital, because otherwise he would probably bleed to death on the street.

"Give me your ID," Mr. Chen said, but Yakup did not react.

178

"You also have to pay 500 yuan as an advance payment. Then I'll examine your wound and decide what to do."

As Halmurat heard what his colleague said, he interposed, "Please, examine him quickly, Chen. The man is bleeding and not totally conscious."

"I just follow the regulations!"

Too often, Halmurat had been annoyed when there was a Uyghur emergency patient and his colleagues considered the regulations more important than their medical care. That's why he worked almost day and night and hardly allowed himself leisure time. Instead of hanging his doctor's coat in the cloakroom, he slipped back to the place where his colleague had left the old man on a waiting seat.

"Show me your wound," he said softly.

Yakup looked up. He did not understand Chinese very well and felt relieved when finally someone spoke with him in his own language.

"Come with me, please. Your wound needs cleaning and sewing. You've already lost a lot of blood, haven't you? How do you feel?"

The old man did not answer. He seemed to be in shock, but when Halmurat took him by the hand, he followed him willingly into a corner of the treatment room.

"What are you doing, Halmurat? The man has no identity card!"

"I'm looking at his wound."

"And he did not pay either! So stop it!"

"Don't you see how much he is bleeding, Chen? We are doctors, we must help..."

"... and he must pay."

"He'll pay for it later. And if he cannot pay, then I'll do it for him."

"..."

"Don't worry, I'll see to it."

"That's against the regulations!"

"So," Halmurat turned to his patient, ignoring the colleague. "Wait a moment, now it will hurt a little, attention... keep quiet ... I have to clean the wound, this is important."

"Idiot!" Halmurat heard Dr. Chen saying to another doctor, but he concentrated on his work, cleaned and sewed the deep laceration, and put a thick white bandage around Yakup's head.

"Can you go home alone?"

Still no answer.

"Well, wait a moment. My work is done for today, I will take you home."

"My cart!"

"I beg your pardon?"

"I must have my cart. I need it. They took it with them."

"Now you come. First, I'll take you home."

As they sat together in Yakup's small room, the old man began to talk. He felt weak and sick and humiliated. Halmurat was happy that he had decided to offer him help. He promised to come again the next day.

"Actually, you needed inpatient treatment," he said as he departed, "but neither of us could have paid for that. Nevertheless you should stay in bed for a few days, because you probably have a concussion and this is not something to joke around with. Your fractured ribs need some rest, too. Can your neighbors look after you?"

Halmurat had a friend who worked for the city's administration and after long and complicated inquiries he succeeded in finding out where Yakup's fruit cart was. Thus, the following evening, a young doctor set out with a three-wheeled handcart loaded with a mountain of food to a small side street in the Uyghur district of Korla. Children played outside and laughed with joy when they saw him, calling out, "Uncle Yakup, Uncle Yakup, your cart is back!"

The old man came to the door and looked out in amazement.

"You should be in bed, Yakup!"

"Yes, sir, I know. I'm going," the old man said, beaming like the sun rising in the morning behind the mountains, when he saw the friendly young man with his old cart. "It suits you, doc, indeed..."

"Off to bed and no argument! First we will look at your wound and then I'll prepare us a nice dinner."

They talked late into the night. Neighbors came and sat down with them. Of course, the whole street knew within a moment that a young doctor had come to visit old Yakup, someone who stood up for the Uyghurs, and everyone wanted to see him and everyone had questions and brought their children and old relatives. It was like a big party, and all the time the convalescent patient sat on his bed, laughing and beaming, something he hadn't done for many years.

"I'll be back," Halmurat promised before he left. "I will come as often as I can, and when your head and ribs and everything have recovered, then we will throw you a big party! Okay?"

They became friends, the young Halmurat and the old Yakup from Korla.

Turap came every morning to the place where he sold his eggs. Every morning he looked at his pocket very carefully to make sure that all the papers were in it. And every morning he hoped that his friend Yakup, the fruit seller, would finally reappear. He had not been able to help him when the police check came. He was ashamed, but what could he have done in the face of their authority? They would have beaten or arrested him too.

One day he came. Turap saw him coming from afar: Yakup with his cart, laden with fruit, pears and dates, so it seemed to him. Yes, of course, the time of yellow figs was long gone. It seemed he had oiled the wheels, for they did not creak. And altogether he looked different. He did not walk with a stoop as usual. And he smiled.

"Good morning, my friend," he greeted the egg seller cheerfully. "How are you?"

"How are *you*, Yakup? I was so worried. It was terrible. I thought you were bleeding to death. I thought you would die in my hands."

"Oh, I'm fine, thank you! I am quite well again," said Yakup gleefully as he piled his pears. "But I've had really great luck. Allah has helped me, because the bleeding did not stop and I really almost died that day... and not in the street, but in the hospital. Right in the middle of the hospital. You won't believe all the things I have to tell you."

"I'm so glad that you're back here. Wait, I got something for you."

Turap pulled from behind his back a crumpled plastic bag and handed it to Yakup with a solemn gesture, "Here, I've kept this for you."

Yakup peeped into the bag curiously.

"My doppa!" he exclaimed in surprise. "Thank you, Turap. I did not think that I'd see it again. That's really nice of you, thank you. Though I have a new one, look here. I got it from my friend... Well, I'll tell you later. Wait, and what is this?"

It was a crushed box with a few bills at the bottom.

"There was not much left when the people were gone." Turap was apologetic. "Children and probably also some adults had collected your money as it flew across the street."

"Ah, my friend!" Yakup had tears in his eyes when he shook hands with his neighbor. "How good to have friends! But wait a moment, I will tell you everything. I have a lot to tell. Come and sit down."

The day was not long enough to talk about all the things the two men had to say.

"And do you know what?" Yakup ended his story. "He said that it had once been his greatest wish to become a heart doctor, you know, a doctor who is specialized in curing hearts. But the hospital did not give him the chance to learn these things. They let him work only in the first aid station – because he is Uyghur – and for many years he had been pretty sad about it. And yet I think he is the best heart doctor you can imagine."

Turap looked at him for a long time.

"Yes, indeed," he mumbled, smiling thoughtfully to himself. "That seems to be true."

Yakup handed one of the remaining pears to the egg seller and said, "We're having a party this evening, my recovery party. Can you come, my friend?"

Hurshida

When Hurshida opened her eyes for the first time, her mother Aynur got a shock. It was like a slap in the face, a blow that hit her with an unexpected vehemence like a flash of lightning in bright sunlight. She suddenly knew with shattering certainty that she had made an irreparable mistake. She had conjured up a disaster that would upset her life and plunge the whole family into misfortune. The ground began to tremble under her feet, as if an earthquake was shaking the earth. As if quicksand was trying to swallow her. She felt betrayed and cheated. She looked again at the child and sank to her knees in despair, unable to think clearly. She sat like this for a long time beside the little creature who was now her daughter.

Hurshida was two weeks old and Aynur for two hours her mother.

Just a few hours ago she had felt as though she was in seventh heaven. She had long ago stopped hoping for a miracle, did not expect her wish to become reality, and yet it had suddenly happened. She had been offered a little girl for adoption, an almost newborn child, about two weeks old, a tiny little creature that needed a mother. And she, Aynur, was to be this mother.

It had been about four o'clock in the afternoon, when the phone had rung. The adoption agency had called and said that they had a little girl for adoption. She had submitted an application some time ago. Was she still interested?

Aynur had nearly dropped the phone and held her breath for a moment. A child... Would her greatest wish come true after all?

"If you are, come and see us! Come at once! Our office closes at five-thirty, as you know," the woman had said, and Aynur had left her desk in the city administration and hurried to the adoption agency in a trance. A daughter... she had always wished to have a daughter! How many years had she longed for a child, a little human being for whom it was worth living. The dream of having her own family – that was a dream she had given up long ago. Her younger siblings no longer needed her and her mother was old. And who knows how long she still had to live. And then, without her mother, she would be all alone in the world. Alone and forlorn. But a child, a little daughter, would stay with her and she could love and care for her forever.

Of course, children ought to have a father, too, but only a *good* father, not just a man who belonged to the family. Marry, no... She would never marry again! She had done so three times and each time it had been a disaster. She would never again rely on a man. Even though an unmarried woman was not very well regarded in Uyghur society, and an unmarried woman with a child, well, she would have to overcome quite a lot of hostility and gossip, but that was better than violence, gambling, and contempt, she had said to herself.

But now? What would happen now? Now that she had a Chinese child, a daughter with slanted eyes, a Han Chinese girl? She who belonged to an old, traditional Uyghur family who had gone through terrible conflicts with the Chinese government years ago. Her father and other relatives had been in jail for a long time because they had expressed their opinions and because the Chinese government did not like their opinions. The fact that there was no real autonomy in the Autonomous Region of Xinjiang, that was a fact that everyone was aware of, but it was not possible to say it in public. Therefore, for Aynur and her family, everything that had to do with politics and injustice meant irresponsible misuse of power, which was synonymous with Han Chinese. Of course, she knew that not all Chinese were bad people, but since those events back then, there was an insurmountable gap between the two ethnic groups.

In the last few years the situation had become even worse. The Uyghurs felt increasingly repressed by the Chinese, treated with contempt, subjugated. And now she had adopted such a child as her daughter! How would she be able to love her? How could she know who her parents were? Maybe they too belonged to those who put the Uyghurs in jail, shot them. Long pent-up resentment, barely acknowledged hatred for the Chinese, suddenly flared up in her and threatened to poison her soul. Ever since Hurshida had opened her eyes, all this half-forgotten animosity had suddenly risen to the surface, and was much, much stronger than ever before.

The door opened and Aynur's mother came in. She had been at the neighbor's and did not yet know what had happened.

"What's the matter with you, Aynur?" she asked in astonishment when she saw her daughter cowering on the kang. She came closer and saw the child lying on the thick felt carpet, wrapped in a colored cloth.

"What's that? A child? Aynur, you have got a child? From the adoption agency? Is it true? All of a sudden, after such a long a time? How... how was it possible, so suddenly?"

"They called me," Aynur answered tonelessly. "They said, 'Take her or leave her!' Then I signed the papers."

"Oh, how wonderful! This is what you've always longed for."

"Yes, I have."

"What a beautiful child! Is it a girl?"

"Yes, a girl. My daughter. But wait until she opens her eyes."

"Why?"

"Do you see the eyelid crease, Mother. Can you see? This is a Chinese child!"

The old woman looked at her daughter in dismay. She did not know what to say. Why had Aynur taken the child, when the family had always been so proud of their origins and had always attached great importance to Uyghur-only marriages and had never mixed with other ethnic groups? Our culture, our traditions, language and religion are our greatest asset, father had always said. We must not jeopardize it by letting ourselves be overrun by Sinicization, and the whole family had agreed, as most Uyghur families in Xinjiang did. And now Aynur had adopted a Chinese child!

"You've already signed the papers? Is the adoption legally binding?"

"Yes."

"Didn't you look at the child?"

"Of course. But she was sleeping. I didn't notice. Not until I got home."

"Maybe you can cancel it. Call them!"

"The office is closed now." Aynur began to cry. "Everything happened so fast. They were all in a hurry, because it was late and nearly time to go home. 'You wanted a daughter, so take her,' they said. 'Otherwise we will give her to another family tomorrow. It's your chance: now or never.' That was it, Mother. I was so excited, I was so incredibly happy that I only cast a quick glance at the little sleeping face and then I signed the documents."

'Now or never,' the employees in the adoption agency had said. She was nearly forty years old and without a husband. They would certainly not ask her a second time. It did occasionally happen that a newborn girl was given up for adoption or even abandoned because her parents wanted a boy instead, and were not allowed to have more than one or two children because of the one-child policy. But most of the women were clever enough to have an abortion if an unwanted girl was on the way. Therefore, Aynur had seized her last and only chance without a second thought, without asking questions.

Now the little girl opened her eyes again, screwed up her face with a feeble grin, turned her head and made clumsy sucking movements with her tiny mouth.

"Did they at least tell you how to feed such a little worm when you have no breast milk?"

Aynur went into the kitchen and prepared a bottle as instructed on the leaflet that they had given her. Hurshida drank eagerly, and then her mother and grandmother began to undress and wash her. Aynur felt a bump on the child's back. She turned her round and got the second shock of the evening. On her spine, just above the tailbone, there was a huge bump.

"Did you get a medical report?" her mother asked.

"No. Why?"

"And what is this here?"

"A bump."

"That's not just a bump. It could be anything. Who knows what diseases this little creature might bring into the house? You must cancel the whole thing, Aynur! They have foisted this child on you because nobody else wants it. After all, who wants a deformed Chinese girl..."

Aynur stared at her mother in horror, asking herself in despair, "Is there a right to return children? Can you return an adopted child like a broken TV or a dress that you bought in the wrong size by mistake? Can you complain and say, 'It is not what I ordered, and anyway it is damaged.'?"

The next morning Aynur went to the adoption agency, described her concerns regarding ethnicity and health, and accused the staff of deliberately deceiving and hurrying her. She had been forced into a hasty decision and wanted to annul the adoption.

"That is absolutely impossible, my good woman." Her request was rejected. "You saw the child and by no means did we force you into signing the adoption papers. It was your own decision and there is nothing we can do about it."

Aynur wept for three days. Hurshida also wept and her grandmother wandered through the house, filled with bitterness. The neighbors came to see the child, they looked at each other and

188

went away. On the third day Aynur pulled herself together, picked up her child and took her to the hospital. The doctor diagnosed a tumor in the lumbar spine. Whether it was benign or malignant, he could not say. They would have to examine her, but in any case, it was better to remove the tumor. Even a benign tumor could affect the function of the spine, hinder growth, cause neurological disorders or pain. At the moment, the child was still too young, but in three to six months she would need an operation.

Now that Aynur knew the facts, she felt a little better. An operation on an infant was risky and also very expensive, but she had no choice. Hurshida was her daughter – even though by fraud – and therefore she was responsible for the little girl, whether she wanted to be or not. Somehow, she had to deal with the consequences of her own rashness and somehow, she would manage! But love... she didn't think she would ever love this Chinese child, whom the neighbors laughed at, who caused her incalculable worries, her mother's anger and immense costs. No, she would not be able to love this child. That dream had gone forever.

"But it's my duty to look after her," she told herself. "It is my duty and I will do everything in my power to raise her with respect so that she will become a good and responsible person."

A few days went by. Aynur tried to spend as much time as possible with her daughter and do everything right. The new life was exhausting: a lot of work, little sleep. Nursing, feeding and changing diapers quickly became routine, but sapped her strength. And the joy of motherhood, which she had once hoped for, failed to materialize.

While the little mouth was sucking on the bottle, Aynur thought back to her first hopes of having a child of her own. She had married early. Her father had promised her to a business friend's son, and as she was an obedient daughter she had said, "If you want me to marry him, Father, I'll marry him, but

I do not know if I can love him." He had replied, "You're still young, my child. Love comes later in marriage." However, it had not come. Neither to her nor to the young man. And when she was still not pregnant after one year, he got impatient, beat her, insulted her. When Aynur was still was not pregnant two years later, he became so unpredictable and violent that she was increasingly afraid of him, and in the third year she applied for a divorce.

A few years later she had married a second time. He had been a friendly young man, polite and courteous and everybody liked him. But again, she did not become pregnant, again the hope of having a child began to fade away, and then one day a doctor told her that she could never be able to conceive. She was infertile. From that day onwards, her husband went out every night. He gambled his money away, lost everything they had. He did not hit her like her first husband, but it was almost worse, because he ignored her, did not even take notice of her any more. She had ceased to exist for him, and so this marriage also ended in divorce.

Hurshida was no longer sucking. She turned her head energetically to one side. Aynur looked at her and thought, "At that time, a little child would have made me happy. Yes, maybe I could even have loved my husband over time. Who knows, maybe we would have become a harmonious family, but now I'm alone and have burdened myself with this child, this strange child."

A few years after the second divorce, Aynur had ventured a third attempt. She had married a widower who brought a child into the marriage. This would solve all her problems, she had thought. She would be a good mother for the child and finally have a real family. But this time, too, everything went wrong. Aynur had not told her husband about her infertility, because she thought that it was no longer of importance. But the man had a daughter and he wanted to have a son. When she confessed the truth to him, he left her. He left without a second glance. He accused her of dishonesty and fraud, filed for divorce, took his child and disappeared from her life.

"I've always done everything wrong," she said aloud.

At this moment, a foot hit her chest. Thin arms paddled aimlessly in the air and bendy baby legs tried to kick off the blanket that was covering them. Hurshida was awake now, replete and content, and she was looking at her mother. Aynur felt her eyes watching her. They were not pretty. No, they were not beautiful Uyghur eyes, but for the first time she saw something in these sparkling, black eyes, which scrutinized her so intently, as if they were trying to memorize her face so that they would never forget it. Stunned, almost alarmed, Aynur became aware of *what* she saw in those eyes: trust. Infinite, boundless and unconditional trust. Curiosity for life. Not gratitude, because for this little creature it seemed to be a natural matter of course that she could rely on her mother. Aynur's eyes moistened, a flow of unknown feelings shot through her whole being, made her shiver, tremble with happiness and emotion, tears dropping onto the bare, thrashing legs. She tenderly stroked the velvety black hair, lifted the child up and gazed for a long time into her slanted eyes.

"So you want to be my daughter, Hurshida? That's what you have just told me, isn't it?" She was sobbing loudly. "Yes, I will be your mom, no matter where you come from, what you look like and how sick you are. I'm your mom and you're my child! I'll do anything for you and no one will separate us. I promise."

It almost looked like a smile. But no, at three weeks a child cannot consciously smile, but maybe it was her soul smiling and making a first attempt to really come to life. Aynur pressed the little creature to her heart, felt at one with her, and knew that she would be able to master all difficulties that lay before her. For herself and for her child. What did it matter whether she was a Chinese or a Uyghur child? People should be there for each other when they need each other, and love can overcome all obstacles if you let it in.

Ten years had passed. Aynur had taken her daughter to school and now stopped for a moment at the gate watching her crossing the schoolyard. Hurshida had grown into a pretty, self-confident girl. She walked a little awkwardly. She lurched slightly and was not able to go long distances without help, but in the past few weeks she had managed at least to walk across the schoolyard without crutches. She looked back and waved to her mother with a smile.

This smile was the bond that had tied them together in all these years and that had eased all the grief. There had been a lot of grief and sorrow. First, there were the neighbors and relatives who were reluctant to accept a Chinese child. There was her mother who had never overcome her rancor against all Han Chinese because they had imprisoned and abused her husband, so that he had returned from jail a broken man and had died shortly after his release. Deep in her heart, she could not forgive her granddaughter for being a descendent of these people. And then the surgery and later countless consultations and therapies that had cost her a fortune. Aynur was deeply in debt, both to her brothers and to the bank. She worked very hard, but even so, she feared that she would never be able to repay the debts. And yet, at this moment when she saw her daughter laughing with her friends as she disappeared into the schoolhouse, she had the feeling that no mother in the whole world could be happier than she was.

She went back to the car, because it was time to go to work. She had had to buy a car, because otherwise it would not have been possible to take her daughter to kindergarten and later to school. At that time, after the operation, the doctors had feared that the child would never learn to walk by herself. Her legs had no strength, had been completely limp. Maybe something had gone wrong during surgery, maybe they had injured a nerve or something else. She did not know and no one provided an explanation. The doctors had just returned her daughter, without the tumor and without life in her legs. At first, she had believed that Hurshida only needed time to recover, but the little legs had never again kicked like they once did when she was a baby.

Aynur had gone to other clinics, had consulted specialists in Kashgar, Hotan and Urumchi. She had tried traditional Uyghur and Chinese medical therapies, but nothing had helped and nobody knew what to do. So Hurshida had learned with infinite patience and great effort over the years to stand on her feet. When she made her first step without help, it had been a day for celebration for both mother and daughter. They had made it! Together, they would manage anything.

As awkward Hurshida was in her movements, her spirit was all the livelier. She was interested in everything and learned fast. Even in kindergarten she spoke fluent Chinese, although at home the family only spoke Uyghur. She knew all the Uyghur and Chinese fairy tales and sang songs in both languages. She played with all children and respected all adults who were kind to her. The only difference she saw in people was not the language, nor the shape of their eyes, but solely whether they were good and accepted her disability or whether they taunted her because of her lame legs. Hurshida bore both cultures in herself and with a tiny smile she had once told her mother that this was not the slightest problem.

"Hurshida, my daughter," Aynur said, as she was driving through heavy traffic to work, "You Chinese girl with a Uyghur heart, you could be key to a peaceful coexistence, if only this torn country would listen to you!"

Glossary

Atlas silk Silk with a typical Uyghur design, reminiscent of flowing water or wood grain

Apa Mother, mom

Bingtuan Chinese shorthand for the Xinjiang Production and Construction Corps, a special Chinese economic and paramilitary unit in Xinjiang

Doppa A square or round skullcap, variously embroidered, which most Uyghur men wear every day, while women wear it only on special occasions

Dotar A traditional long-necked two-stringed lute

Han Chinese This is the term for ethnic Chinese. Of course all citizens of China are Chinese, including the ethnic minorities, but in this book "Chinese" is used only for the ethnic Han Chinese.

Kang A traditional platform for general living, working, entertaining and sleeping, which can be heated from below

Mu Chinese square measure: 1 hectare = 15 mu

Naan bread Oven-baked flatbread, found everywhere in Central Asia and India

Uncle Kurban Kurban Tulum was a Uyghur peasant from a village between Hotan and Keriya. When the People's Liberation Army had made an end to the political turmoil in Xinjiang in 1949, Kurban was so grateful that he set out with his donkey cart to Urumchi, 1500 km away, to give a melon to Mao Zedong. Party officials, seeing in it a public relations sensation, sent him to Beijing where he was allowed to shake hands with the great Chairman.

Sangza Fried noodles, woven into decorative circles

Supa A platform, similar to the kang, mostly made of wood and covered with carpets or mats, serving as living room; it is not heatable from below like the kang.

Tonur Oven made of clay or mud brick

Tugure Small dumplings filled with a minced meat mixture and cooked in boiling water

Yuan Chinese currency (other name: Renminbi): 100 Yuan = 16 US dollars

Epilogue to the 2015 Edition

Why did I write all of these stories? In wanted to tell people in western countries something about the Uyghurs, because there is still so little known about their sad situation in Xinjiang, and because I have great sympathy for these people whom I myself know as patient, warmhearted and extremely hospitable. In China, however, they are under general suspicion of being violent terrorists or separatists who endanger state security. And if there are occasionally reports in the international media, it is mostly in such a context. With these stories, I wanted to show what the situation is really is like. I wanted my readers to understand the Uyghurs and their feelings. I wanted to stir up people.

Of course, there are among Uyghurs some hotheads and extremists as there are in every nation and every country. Moreover, there are other and even more violent regimes than China's, and there are ethnic groups that are treated more cruelly than the Uyghurs in Xinjiang, but nonetheless they are among the most endangered peoples of the world and that should not be.

In fact, it should not be even under the Chinese system, because the Constitution of the People's Republic of China guarantees equal rights to all ethnic minorities. Although the Uyghurs are no longer allowed to call their country "East Turkistan," because this name recalls the days of sovereignty, according to the law, they have the right to self-governance in matters of economics, science, culture, art, religion and language. The laws are good, but the government does not comply with them, in Xinjiang even less than in the rest of China, and in recent years the situation has worsened. Conflicts between Chinese security forces and the local Uyghur community are increasing, including a high number of arrests of Uyghurs on the charge of "endangering state security." It may be that there are some

Uyghurs acting as aggressors, but no one ever explains *why* these incidents occur, how much they have been humiliated, cheated or provoked.

The government does nothing to ease the situation. Instead of democratic reforms, President Xi Jinping has imposed even more persecution, intimidation, arbitrary arrests, unfair trials, and long prison sentences of human rights defenders. The number of killed people during politically motivated violence in Xinjiang is now much higher than in Tibet.

The stories in this book cannot help the Uyghurs in Xinjiang, but they can draw attention to their situation and show how much they are worthy of respect.

Epilogue to the 2021 Edition

When Party Secretary Chen Quanguo was transferred to Xinjiang at the end of 2016, he immediately began to implement his surveillance concept, tried and tested in Tibet, on an even larger scale and with more modern means. New police stations were built on nearly every street corner. Video surveillance with facial recognition software, DNA samples, mobile phone apps and the like soon ensured seamless mass surveillance and the arbitrary arrest of hundreds of thousands of Uyghurs and members of other Muslim minorities. As early as 2017, huge complexes sprang up across the country, the so-called "re-education camps", because all prisons had long been overcrowded. For a long time, the Chinese government vehemently denied the existence of such camps. But when satellite images finally showed the world where and how big they were, it was claimed that they were training centers where students learned wonderful things and were happy. The camps were cordoned off over a large area, journalists were not given access, and since from then on any contact with relatives or friends in foreign countries was extremely dangerous for the Uyghurs, there were hardly any reliable eyewitness reports.

In November 2019, the „China Cables" were disclosed, confidential documents of the Communist Party, including detailed instructions on the operation of the detention camps and information on surveillance databases, which proved that all these suppressive measures were being carried out at the express instructions of Xi Jinping and the central government in Beijing: The Uighurs should finally and forever lose their ethnic identity, forget their language, culture, religion, their thinking and their self-respect.

The Stories

ll stories in this book are based on real events. The names and most places have been changed to protect the persons concerned, and some details have been added or omitted. Nevertheless, each story relates true experiences.

I thank all those who have told me about their lives, and those who told me what their friends or relatives could not tell me.

My special thanks go to the authors of the website "*kechmish we eslime*" (life and memories) of Radio Free Asia (http://www.rfa.org/uyghur/yoruq-sahillar), who drew my attention to some of the cases.

What happened when?
Murat 2003, Ghalip 2010, Hamut 2009, Kurbanjan 2009, Rozihan 2013, Nurgul 2010, Abdurahman 2014, Gulmira 2005, Yanar 2011, Burhanidin 2013-2014, Filora 2006, Amangul 2014, Halmurat 2013, Hurshida 2004 and 2014

Afterword

Cover Photo

This photo was taken by the author in Kashgar in summer 2011, near the Id Kha Mosque. Uyghurs are walking in front of a military demonstration of the Chinese People's Liberation Army.

Ghalip

After July 2009, internet surveillance was drastically tightened and since then, imprisoned Uyghur human rights defenders have included many bloggers and journalists.
http://www.gfbv.de/uploads/download/download/283.pdf

Nurgul

Ten persons had been killed and two injured girls imprisoned. No one in the village knew the reason for this massacre, but everywhere in Xinjiang there are occasional violent conflicts. It can be caused by police forcibly shaving a man's beard or taking away a woman's scarf, or some big or small outrage which makes accumulated grievances explode. Some Uyghurs, especially young men, see no means of defending themselves than attacking an official or a police station. These excesses are brutally repressed and interpreted as terroristic acts.

Abdurahman

A young man had captured video of the protest march with his mobile phone and posted it on the internet. A few hours later, the video was deleted and the whole district was cut off from internet access. It happens quite frequently in Xinjiang that entire towns or regions are cut off from internet access for several days, sometimes for weeks or even months, because the government is afraid that such incidents will spark demonstrations or further violence. The Aksu district government's website, however, remained available and one could read there that Abdurahman Ablimit was a terrorist.

Burhanidin

Burhanidin (whose real name is not Burhanidin) and his friends were sentenced in August 2014 to 18 to 24 months imprisonment and high penalties because of "illegally raising funds". However, after his partners appealed against the judgement and international groups intervened, they were released early, in November 2014.

Amangul

Everywhere in China there are from time to time protests by village communities whose land has been seized by officials of the local government to make huge profits by paying the farmers paltry compensation and selling the land to investors who offer gigantic sums. These protests often escalate into violent clashes with the police and they normally end with imprisonment for the farmers. This happens all over China, but in Xinjiang, ethnic conflict exacerbates the problem, because the farmers are Uyghurs and the officials – at least those who are powerful enough to carry off these schemes – are Han Chinese.

The Sheep

Fat-tailed sheep are an old domestic breed which has most likely existed for around 6,000 years. They are highly appreciated by the Uyghurs, because not only is their flesh is particularly lean and delicate, but also their fat is tasty and good for health. The fat-tailed sheep save a large part of their body fat in the fat tail, similar to the camels in their humps. This stored fat is much softer in consistency than other fat. (see: https://en.wiki-pedia.org/wiki/Fat-tailed_sheep)

books in this series:

#Uyghur Stories
#In the land of the Uyghurs
#Aliya and the little dog

Ingrid Widiarto was born in Schleswig in 1947. She grew up in Kiel, graduated in Germersheim as a translator for Romance languages and worked as a translator and secretary, for many years at the Free University of Berlin.

Through family and traveling she got to know different countries and cultures, and when she learnt about the precarious living conditions of the Uyghurs in worthwest China, it upset her so much that she set herself the task of drawing attention to it. So she began to write books und stories and to maintain a website:

https://www.uigurkultur.com/

VERLAG
AKADEMIE DER ABENTEUER

neugierig • grenzenlos • unterhaltsam

Unser Verlagsname basiert auf den gleichnamigen Büchern des Autors Boris Pfeiffer. In dessen zeit- und welterforschender Reihe „Akademie der Abenteuer" sind es Reisen der Protagonisten in die Vergangenheit, die für viele LeserInnen ein Erlebnis geworden sind, Kinder und Erwachsene gleichermaßen.

Im *Verlag Akademie der Abenteuer* wird die Erforschung der Welt mit den Mitteln der Literatur fortgesetzt. AutorInnen und ZeichnerInnen, DichterInnen und MalerInnen arbeiten in der Akademie der Abenteuer zusammen.

Reisen in den Geist, erkenntnisreich, selbstbewusst, gut erzählt, sind der Kern des Verlagsprogramms.

Im *Verlag Akademie der Abenteuer* entstehen Bilderbücher, Kinderbücher, Kinderbuchreihen und Jugendliteratur. Wir veröffentlichen packend erzählte Gegenwartsliteratur. Weiteres Augenmerk legen wir auf Kunstbände, in denen Malerei und Dichtung neue Felder eröffnen. Zweisprachige Ausgaben und ungewöhnliche Blicke in die Welt, sowie Lehr- und Sachbücher runden unser Programm ab.

Mehr auf unserer Website:
www.verlagakademie.de

GUDRUN WIEBKE - KOMISSAR TRAUDICH

... und das Schweigen des Stoppelfelds

„Ist es nicht so, dass jedem kriminalistischen Triumph das Versagen einer ganzen Welt vorausgeht?"
In Traudichs Augen standen Zweifel.
„Einer ganzen Welt?", fragte Anton vorsichtig zurück.

Immer wenn Traudich einen Fall abgeschlossen hatte, tat sich im Kommissar von Eiderstedt dieses Loch auf, in das er abzustürzen drohte. Und wenn Anton seinen Freund dann nicht stoppte, folgte die Selbstbezichtigung, weil genau dieses Versagen der ganzen Welt seinen komfortablen Lebensstandard sicherte.

Kommissar Traudich
Kriminalerzählungen
ISBN-13 (Print): 978-3-98530-012-9
ISBN-13 (Ebook): 978-3-98530-013-6

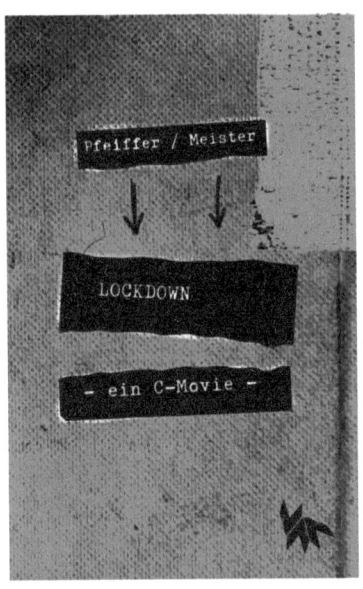

Lockdown - ein C-movie

Michèle Meister & Boris Pfeiffer

Showdown im Lockdown. Heulen, kämpfen, hell und düster denken, auf und ab im C-Leben in C-Zeiten als C-Movie aus den Straßen Berlins und Melbournes. Was abgeht, wenn das Menschengeschlecht nicht mehr on top of the world ist, krasse Knastnummer, Krokodilstränen, freizischende Seelenrakete in den Himmel. Der erste Bild- und Gedichtband der in Australien arbeitenden und lebenden Malerin Michèle Meister und des Berliner Autors Boris Pfeiffer ist visuell und inhaltlich ein Werk von großer Kraft.

Lockdown - ein C-Movie
ISBN-13 (Print): 978-3-98530-002-0
ISBN-13 (Ebook): 978-3-98530-003-7

DIE BOOTSBAUER - FELIX HUBY

Julius Kommerell hat es geschafft. Vom mittellosen Lehrling ist er zum Leiter der Firma Steininger Bootsbau aufgestiegen und hat die Tochter Doris Steininger, einziges Kind des Firmengründers, geheiratet. Die beiden haben inzwischen zwei erwachsene Kinder. Kommerell arbeitet an einem Boot, das die Krönung seiner vielen erfolgreichen Entwicklungen werden soll. Aber da setzt ihm seine Frau, die alleinige Besitzerin des Unternehmens, plötzlich den Stuhl vor die Tür und erklärt sich zur alleinigen Chefin der Werft. Für Julius Kommerell bricht eine Welt zusammen. Er verlässt Firma und Familie, zieht in sein Bootshaus am jenseitigen Ufer des Sees und muss von dort aus hilflos zusehen, wie Doris und sein Sohn Florian *Steininger Bootsbau* in die Krise steuern. Da hat er einen Plan...

Die Bootsbauer
Ein Bodenseeroman
ISBN-13 (Print): 978-3-98530-000-6
ISBN-13 (Ebook): 978-3-98530-001-3

AKADEMIE DER ABENTEUER - BORIS PFEIFFER
Kris Kersting Illustrationen

„Akademie des leibhaftigen Studiums vergangener Zeiten" – Rufus' neue Schule hat es in sich, im wahrsten Sinne des Wortes: Sie steckt voller rätselhafter Fundstücke aus der Vergangenheit und jedes Teil birgt Geheimnisse. Um diese zu lüften, braucht es besondere Fähigkeiten …

Zusammen mit seinen Freunden Fili, No und der Bisamratte Minster stürzt sich Rufus in die neuen Fächer: „Antike Schwertkunde", „Speisen aus allen Jahrtausenden" und „Vergessene olympische Disziplinen". Aber das ist nur der Anfang. Schon bald durchströmen längst vergessene Szenen aus der Zeit der Pharaonen die Akademie …

Leserstimmen:

„Es gibt Kinderbücher, welche nur für Kinder gedacht und geeignet sind. Dann gibt es noch solche, die mich als Erwachsene noch fesseln können. Dazu gehört „Die Akademie der Abenteuer" von Boris Pfeiffer. (Tines Bücherwelt)

„Boris Pfeiffer gelingt es mit detailreicher Sprache, von der ersten bis zur letzten Seite Hochspannung zu schaffen." (Lesewelt Ortenau)

„Ein starker Auftakt zu einer genialen Jugendbuchreihe, die es so noch nicht gegeben hat. Eine Reise in die Vergangenheit, die für Jung und Alt ein Erlebnis ist, das man so schnell nicht vergisst!" (liesundlausch.de)

„Was für eine Serie! Es lebe "Die Akademie der Abenteuer"! Eine so wunderbare Verbindung von historisch packendem Stoff mit liebenswerten Charakteren und spannender Handlung sucht ihresgleichen. Hier gilt auf alle Fälle: Nicht entgehen lassen und sofort zugreifen!" (Leserwelt)

Band 1
Die Knochen der Götter
ISBN-13 (Print): 978-3-98530-004-4
ISBN-13 (Ebook): 978-3-98530-005-1

Band 2
Die Stunde des Raben
ISBN-13 (Print): 978-3-98530-006-8
ISBN-13 (Ebook): 978-3-98530-007-5

Band 3
Das Schiff aus Stein
ISBN-13 (Print): 978-3-98530-008-2
ISBN-13 (Ebook): 978-3-98530-009-9

Band 4
Das Erbe des Rings
ISBN-13 (Print): 978-3-98530-010-5
ISBN-13 (Ebook): 978-3-98530-011-2